D1554874

AND THE RIVER RAN RED

OTHER FIVE STAR NOVELS
BY ROD MILLER

A Thousand Dead Horses
Pinebox Collins
Father unto Many Sons
Rawhide Robinson Rides a Dromedary:
The True Tale of a Wild Camel Cabellero
Rawhide Robinson Rides the Tabby Trail:
The True Tale of a Wild West CATastrophe
Rawhide Robinson Rides the Range:
True Adventures of Bravery and Daring in the Wild West

AND THE RIVER RAN RED

A NOVEL OF THE
MASSACRE AT BEAR RIVER

ROD MILLER

FIVE STAR
A part of Gale, a Cengage Company

LIBRARY OF CONGRESS CATALOGING-IN-PUBLICATION DATA

Names: Miller, Rod, 1952- author.
Title: And the river ran red : a novel of the massacre at Bear
  River / Rod Miller.
Description: First edition. | Waterville, Maine : Five Star, 2021.
Identifiers: LCCN 2021011534 | ISBN 9781432878863 (hardcover)
Subjects: LCSH: Bear River Massacre, Idaho, 1863—Fiction. |
  GSAFD: Historical fiction. | Western stories.
Classification: LCC PS3613.I55264 A84 2021 | DDC 813/.6—dc23
LC record available at https://lccn.loc.gov/2021011534

First Edition. First Printing: September 2021
Find us on Facebook—https://www.facebook.com/FiveStarCengage
Visit our website—http://www.gale.cengage.com/fivestar
Contact Five Star Publishing at FiveStar@cengage.com

Printed in Mexico
Print Number: 01   Print Year: 2022

Dedicated to the Northwestern Band of the Shoshone Nation, victims of the most horrendous massacre of American Indians by the U.S. Army in the history of the West, but who have survived to live productive and noble lives.

Their dying groans rose hideous as the sword smote them,
and the river ran red with blood.

—*The Iliad* of Homer

Continuing with unflinching courage for over four hours you completely cut him to pieces, captured his property and arms, destroyed his stronghold, and burned his lodges.

—Colonel Patrick Edward Connor,
United States Army

Men, who took part in that battle, boast today of taking little infants by the heels and beating their brains out on any hard substance they could find.

—Be-shup,
Shoshoni survivor

FOREWORD

My love affair with words began at such a young age that I don't recall a life without some form of poetry, be it song or spoken word. My mother listened to the great singer/songwriters of the folk scare, the likes of Gordon Lightfoot, John Denver, Marty Robbins, and Judy Collins. When I first heard Ian Tyson's *Cowboyography*—the album that both revived his career and capstoned a revival of western culture—I had no idea that he was the same Ian Tyson from my mother's record collection that included "Ian & Sylvia."

A high school creative-writing teacher and author, Margaret Rostkowski, suggested I take in some Robert Frost and Robert Service poetry. I was about fifteen years old and had also recently discovered Bruce Kiskaddon, S. Omar Barker, Larry McWhorter, Baxter Black, Waddie Mitchell, and a score of other cowboy and cowlady poets from the golden and contemporary West.

It is through the literature that stirred my soul that I have sought the Real West. The one you don't see from the interstate highways. I must fairly admit that the history of my home state of Utah and the Great American West played as big a role for setting me on the course of my life as a singer/songwriter.

So how did I miss the Bear River Massacre? Surely the history teachers from my formative years knew of this dark chapter in Utah, Idaho, and American History. I remember Mountain Meadows—not from Sunday school, but from my seventh grade

Utah history class. It was a hard discovery for me and every LDS-reared classmate around me.

I got the Donner Party.

I got the Goodnight-Loving Trail.

I got the gold rushes, the vaqueros, the transition to fenced rangeland, the transition to the role of the pickup truck in agriculture, the dust-bowl era, the Great Depression, and the surge of corporate ranching in the Great Basin that fostered the buckaroo culture that every wannabe like me longs to be a part of.

But I mostly missed the Bear River Massacre. Did I just not pay attention that day? Was the story so dark to me as a young student that I pushed it out of my memory and subconscious? How could I be born and raised in the very place that I would choose, had I consciously been able to, surrounded by native Shoshone land, and not know the significance of the Bear River Massacre and the story and struggle of The People?

Until Rod Miller came along, generously befriended me, and in better trust than I deserve sent me a poem that stirred my soul every bit as much as "The Ballad of Sam McGhee," "The Road Less Traveled," or "The Man from Snowy River."

It was called "And the River Ran Red. . . ."

In the midst of a short stint back home between road trips packed with performances and interviews, I gave the work a quick read. Many times a seasoned writer had invited me to write music to their verse not knowing the complexity of such a request.

I read the poem again. The unmistakable chill of poetic magic sent a warm shiver down my spine. My throat swelled and my heart warmed and paced up to meet the rush of fresh discovery that came not just from the brilliance of the work but the tragedy of the tale.

And still I resisted.

I shut the computer, pulled on my boots, and started down the gravel two-track to the barn to complete the nagging chores that, in such a limited amount of time, felt unmanageable.

Then the melody began to haunt me.

And the river ran red, rolling with the bodies of the dead. A five minor chord shift from a six minor progression.

"Am I really hearing this now, this way?"

The images of my fallen Shoshone brothers and sisters holding their bleeding children flashed through my mind as the tune developed further.

A strong four chord to start a bridge that needed nothing more than a little shift of already masterfully written lyrics. . . .

By the time I had abandoned my chores and made it back to the house to pick up my guitar and reopen my computer the music was all but written. The melody came faster than my feeble hands and mind could harness it. I don't recall how long I spent fleshing and arranging but it had to be less than an hour and I never broke a sweat. These are the moments artists live for and sometimes even more thrilling and meaningful in the form of a collaboration. Particularly with an accomplished and respected author the likes of Rod Miller.

The experience has allowed me to perform the song at the annual Bear River Massacre commemorations in 2019 and 2020. From a makeshift stage I sing these words and play these chords while looking into the eyes of the very ancestors of those that perished that dark day in January of 1863. The former chairman of the Northwest Band of the Shoshone Nation, Darren Parry, is now a dear friend. The People, and their struggle, are now real for me.

And the Bear River Massacre is now a historical event that will never again be lost upon me. The high and lonesome places I love—Wyoming, Idaho, Utah, Nevada—no longer constitute the land of my birthright, but rather the land of the native

Shoshone. And regardless of right or privilege, I better damn well be a good steward.

How honored I am to write this Foreword. To know The People even just a little better. To recalibrate my perspective of the sacred land that I have been so in love with all my life. To be so moved by the accurate depiction of a dark event in history that I am compelled to teach my children to always find ways to unify, love, and serve.

There is poetic license in this work. But believe me when I tell you that Rod Miller is inspired by God to tell the story in a way that you will never forget.

You will see the California Volunteers ache for water on the march across the Great Basin. You will see a community of Shoshone working together to provide for each other. You will feel Brigham Young's disdain for the US Army and government. You will learn a lot about the geography of Nevada, Utah, and southern Idaho. If you've always seen Porter Rockwell as a larger-than-life, legendary character with a sedulous loyalty to the Mormon faith and a ruthless will to protect it, you will feel with him an unspeakable sadness that reveals a vulnerability you may never know he had.

You will take a desperate ride through hellfire with Sagwitch.

Most important, you will likely see the American Indian, the Shoshone, The People, as the human brother or sister that they were then in 1863, are now, and will always be. And I solidly bet that you will put this book down when it's finished with a desire to find common ground with those that you believe oppose you if only to prevent the atrocities like this dark event in history from ever happening again.

But steel yourself for the sojourn of the read, for Rod Miller, much like a Shoshone warrior fighting for his homeland, means to pierce your heart with an arrow of truth.

—Brenn Hill

www.brennhill.com

14

PROLOGUE

9 June 1878

Porter Rockwell squinted and scowled his way out of fitful sleep, slung his feet over the side of the squalid cot, and struggled to sit upright. Even as chills gripped him, his long beard and longer hair were tangled and sticky with sweat. Sick to his stomach, he could not get a breath, and his heart pounded. He struggled into his boots and collapsed back onto the clammy blankets from the effort.

He would not rise again.

On this, the ninth day of June in the year 1878, the day of his death, Rockwell had been a Mormon—a member of the Church of Jesus Christ of Latter-day Saints—longer than any man alive. He had been there the day of its beginning and every day since. And no man, regardless of tenure, was ever more loyal or obedient to the faith and its leaders.

He had served near half a century along a thin edge separating the lawful and the lawless. At the behest of his superiors, he had arrested and jailed men as a lawman. And he himself had been arrested and jailed as an outlaw.

And he had killed.

In reporting his demise, the *Salt Lake Tribune* accused Rockwell of "at least a hundred murders for the Church," then went on to claim the man was:

Brutal in his instincts, lawless in his habits, and a fanatical devotee of the Prophet [whose word] he received as the will of the Lord, and with the ferocity born of mistaken zeal, he grew to believe that the most acceptable service he could render the Almighty was, as Lear expresses it, to 'kill, kill, kill, kill, kill!' . . . The Danite Rockwell retired from the avenging business and for some years past has been extensively engaged in raising horses and cattle. But the recollection of his evil deeds haunted him, and his conscience preyed upon his soul like the undying worm.

As he lay dying it was not the deaths of the "unsuspecting travelers, fellow saints who held secrets, apostates who dared wag their tongues, mere sojourners in Zion he killed merely to keep his hand in" of which the newspaper accused him that roiled in Rockwell's mind.

Rather, it was images of scarlet streams steaming on white snow, puddling in sticky clay, trickling on shattered ice, swirling in gray water.

It was a dead woman, little more than a girl, caved-in head leaking milky fluid clotted by cold and matted in her black hair, sliced open chest to crotch, disemboweled into the mud, her body mingled with the gore of a mangled baby butchered just a few weeks shy of his impending birth.

It was the sizzle and stink of a heated bayonet, pulled from flames of kindled lodges and thrust into the old man, ear through ear.

It was a soldier, pants around his ankles, atop a Shoshoni woman even as her life leaked away through wounds inflicted by that selfsame soldier.

It was a young man struggling strong up a clay embankment through a storm of lead, perforated by a dozen bullets and more before sliding back down in a red smear of death.

It was a child bobbing down the icy river in a wake of tears and blood and bubbling screams.

And it was the cold.

Never again had Porter Rockwell felt cold so deep in his bones, until the cold that gripped him on his deathbed—a chill caused, maybe, by memories of that day long past—but, maybe, caused by fear of the dark, deep, endless cold soon to come.

CHAPTER ONE

August 1862

Like fleets of stone ships sailing seas of sand and sagebrush and saltgrass and alkali go the mountains of Nevada. Distance undulates on heat waves of late August, reality shimmering, shifting, unsteady.

Softly, across the dry wastes, floats misplaced music from a military band, rippling, streaming, swimming now on the surface, now submerged, disappearing only to appear, disappear, reappear in turn. Then comes cadence—rhythmic pounding of footstep and hoofbeat punctuated by the bitten-off bark of marching orders controlling the pulse and flow.

It is Sunday. Colonel Patrick Edward Connor admires his California Volunteers at dress parade. Somewhere in the desolation on the way to their assignment to build forts to protect the overland routes, the telegraph line, the emigrant trails, they drill.

Major Edward McGarry sits horseback under intense desert sun. His appearance mirrors that of all the troops: red-rimmed eyes, cracked lips, skin dry and peeling, hair brittle and lank. His thoughts are not on this present farce, in which he participates mechanically. Nor is his mind occupied with his cotton mouth, parched throat, or roiling stomach aslosh with bad water. He does not think of ninety miles of barren desert crossed over three long days with temperatures topping one hundred and twenty degrees. Or of the identical days and miles still to come.

He thinks, instead, of a place on the western slope of the Sierra. A place where, just weeks ago, a man with a wagon, a merchant with goods for sale, approached the column. The wares he carried were dear to McGarry's heart: a full load of whiskey. And he thinks of how Connor rewarded the man for his offer: lashed to a hind wheel of his wagon and whipped, while spilled whiskey from ax-split barrels soaked into the soil like so many shed tears.

These are the thoughts of Major Edward McGarry, sitting horseback in the sun in the Nevada desert on a Sunday on the way to nowhere, in parade dress.

But McGarry sheds no tears. For, while the losses of that day could never be regained, Colonel Connor is not all knowing, and all is not lost. Oh, the colonel knew, surely, about the incident shortly after the destruction of the drink, in which a wayside saloon was robbed of its entire store of liquor. And Connor attacked the resulting possibility of whiskey in the ranks by lining up the entire command for canteen inspection. But Colonel Connor cannot be everywhere, and he cannot see everything, and he cannot know all.

So it is that Edward McGarry is able to face the absurdity of dress parade in the middle of the desert in the middle of nowhere with ambivalence, fortified as he is with sufficient whiskey for this day and the days ahead.

CHAPTER TWO

September 1862

Among all the mountain ranges in all the world there is, perhaps, none as remarkable as the Ruby Mountains of Nevada Territory. "The Alps of America" they are called by some. But the Alps of Europe do not rise unannounced from the barren flats of the Great Basin as the Ruby Mountains do, to tower eleven thousand feet and more into an azure sky pure and unfiltered by the haze of humidity. And so they stand razor edged against the sky, the craggy peaks sharpened rather than softened by the snow that clings in the shaded cracks and crevices for most of a year.

At the southeastern verge of the range lies Ruby Marsh, what passes for an oasis in this dry territory. And near that oasis was a trading post and a Pony Express station refitted to serve the Overland Mail and Stage. The transcontinental telegraph also passed this way. Near here, Colonel Connor established Fort Ruby, adjacent to the Overland route and within striking distance of the California Trail along the Humboldt River fifty miles north of the place.

A few men can appreciate the harsh and horrible beauty of such places. Most cannot. The distance, the emptiness, the dryness, the heat, the cold, the dust, the wind, the monotony, the monochromatic landscape overwhelm. Fort Ruby, which Connor and his soldiers established in the barrens, would soon and ever after be known among soldiers as the "worst place in the West."

Upon arrival, Connor put the troops to work with axes and saws and shovels, hauling logs from the mountains and putting up the buildings that would be the fort. Presently, the commander changed into civilian clothes and hitched a ride on a mail coach to Salt Lake City for some clandestine intelligence gathering.

In his absence, realization grew among the troops of the reality of their situation. The California Volunteers, to the man, had volunteered to fight secessionists. This sweating in the construction trades by day, and freezing around sagebrush fires by night, was not to their liking. Nor was the prospect of service in Utah Territory—the prospect faced by most of the troops— any more intriguing to these volunteer soldiers with a yen for action.

Dissatisfaction grew in the ranks, and complainants congregated, grousing men grouped together in gangs whose arguments radiated as much heat as the desert sun. Solutions were debated, strategies thrashed out, tactics considered, diplomacy discussed. Thus, upon his return from Salt Lake City, Connor was met by an unhappy Major McGarry representing discontented troops.

McGarry, well aware of course of the colonel's contrary nature, attacked with stealth and subterfuge. He allowed the commander time to settle in and recover from the road before requesting an audience, during which he circled his subject rather than broaching it directly.

"How was the trip, Colonel? I trust you encountered no difficulties on the road."

"Only boredom and discomfort, Major McGarry. It amazes me that anyone would, or could, man one of those infernal mail coaches and travel this bleak land day after day. It would drive me to insanity.

"All along the way one believes the Paiute and Shoshoni to be about. And one is given to believe the Mormon Militia has protection of the road well in hand. We shall have to see about that—asking the fox to guard the chickens, if you ask me."

"How did you find Salt Lake City?"

"The city is better than I expected, I must confess. A clean and orderly place, well situated at the foot of a beautiful mountain range. The people . . . now that's another story. Like pets, they are, pets of Brigham Young. Nothing happens there without his blessing, and anything that happens against his wishes results in harsh punishment at the hands of his henchmen.

"And old men with long whiskers walk the public streets with two, three, and more wives—many quite comely—marching behind. Disgusting! That lecherous old men would force marriage and their affections on young and unsuspecting girls is wickedness itself.

"Furthermore, I doubt the loyalty of the Mormons to the Union. They pay it lip service, but their sincerity is questionable. All in all, a horrible bunch of people. Here, let me read from my report." Connor shuffled through the papers on his field desk to locate a draft of the official dispatch to his superiors. "How did I put it? Let's see . . . aah, here it is: 'a community of traitors, murderers, fanatics, and whores,' is how I said it. Pointed words, McGarry, but I believe them, every one.

"So I have opted not to billet the troops at Camp Floyd—Fort Crittenden, if you'd rather—that the rebel turncoat Albert Sydney Johnston established during the Utah Expedition. The place is good for nothing but grazing, and it's too far from Salt Lake City. I have selected, instead, a site on benchlands just east of the city. Our presence there will ever remind Brigham

Young and his Mormons to behave themselves."

Connor allowed McGarry to mull that one over for a moment before asking, "How have things here been in my absence, Major? It appears the construction work has been going forward."

"Yes, sir, it has."

"Come on then, McGarry, spit it out. I can see you've something on your mind."

"Well, sir, it's the men. They are unhappy, sir."

"And what is it that's not to their liking?"

"It's a long list, sir. But it all comes down to the idea that we're here in this godforsaken place, with most of us on our way to Utah Territory, instead of going back east to fight the war. That's what the men signed up to do, Colonel, not put up buildings, or wait for dirty Indians to misbehave, or babysit a bunch of damned Mormons."

Connor laughed long and hard.

"What is so funny, Colonel? Those are the men's sentiments, I assure you. You've no cause to scoff at their wishes."

"I understand," Connor said, controlling his laughter. "I laugh only because I share those sentiments. I have driven my superiors to distraction haranguing them with requests to deploy the California Volunteers elsewhere. They have all but charged me with insubordination. So, I fear, you will have to inform the men there is nothing to be done, at least for the time being. If need be, and if conditions merit, we shall seek our glory fighting Indians rather than the rebels."

"If the savages would show themselves, that is."

"They will, Major McGarry, they will. The Shoshoni are quiet for now, but it will not last, if history is any indicator."

"Be that as it may, Colonel, the men have a plan."

"What might that be?"

"We have all agreed to donate from our pay thirty thousand

24

dollars to the Army—if the Army will use that money to transport us to Virginia."

Connor considered for a moment what McGarry had told him. "First of all, Major McGarry, let me say that I have absolutely no hope that this offer will be accepted. Even so, I will forward the proposal by wire to General Halleck, himself, in Washington, over my signature. Furthermore, I will strongly recommend—despite my misgivings, which shall remain private—that the government accept Brigham Young's offer of continued protection of the Overland Mail route with members of the Mormon militia, in order that the Volunteers may be free for reassignment in the East."

"The men will be pleased, sir."

"Not so fast, Major; you must also inform the men that, if the Army does not see fit to accept their offer, they are to perform the duties assigned without further grousing. Any discipline problems will be punished surely and severely. Am I clear?"

"Yes, Colonel. I will inform the men."

Headquarters received the telegram as promised but, as expected, refused to change the orders. The California Volunteers were compelled to draw their pay and serve out the terms of their enlistments in the Great Basin, far away from the bloody battlefields of the War of the Rebellion.

Even so, there would be blood enough for the California Volunteers.

And it started to flow just days later, with the arrival of a wire at Fort Ruby telling of the recent killing of an emigrant party at a place called Gravelly Ford on the Humboldt. There were insufficient troops at Fort Churchill at present to investigate or retaliate.

Connor replied by wire: "Will attend to it."

CHAPTER THREE

Had the ball from a well-aimed cannon landed where Porter Rockwell was sitting, it would have substantially eliminated the leadership of the Mormon church. President Brigham Young, his counselors, and assistants—and most of the members of the Quorum of the Twelve Apostles—huddled in a room too small for the purpose.

Because of the crowd and because daytime temperatures in Utah Territory often reach uncomfortably high levels even in late September, the room was so stuffy as to be stifling. Besides, Rockwell was never at ease in such situations. He would rather have given his report personally to Brigham Young, as was the usual order of things, but in the interest of economy the president had asked Rockwell to attend the meeting so the entire leadership could be enlightened at once.

Brother Brigham invited one of the apostles to pray, then got right to business. "Brethren," he said, "you see that Brother Porter Rockwell is among us. You all know Port. I've asked him to join us as he has been doing a little snooping around on my behalf and has information about the army and its intentions. So, before we take up our agenda, we shall hear what he has to say. Just go ahead on, Port. We don't stand on ceremony here."

Rockwell did not rise from his seat or move to the head of the room. Rather, his high-pitched, squeaky voice addressed the assembled prophets, seers, and revelators from a seat near the door at the side of the room.

"Well, gents, as you know we been hearing rumors since as far back as June that the government back in Washington intended to replace our militia troops watching the Overland Mail route and the telegraph line with soldiers of their own," Rockwell began.

The only other sound in the room was the scratching of a clerk's pen. From before the days of its formal organization, the Latter-day Saints' church was hell-bent on record keeping, and scribes were appointed to record everything down to and including the most mundane minutiae.

But not this time. Brigham Young interrupted Rockwell and said, "Port, let me break in here to inform the clerk that your remarks needn't be recorded." The pen fell silent. "Go ahead on."

"So, anyways, that's what they've done. They've raised volunteer troops out of California, and they've been making their way here since July. Just now the whole passel of them is in Ruby Valley, where they stopped to build a fort."

"Is it possible that they will stay there?"

"I don't believe so, Brig."

"Surely they can guard the road from there as well as anyplace."

"Could do. But they won't. See, the man in charge is a fellow named Patrick Edward Connor. Colonel Connor, now. He used to be a captain in the regular army and fought in the Mexican War but gave it up and went to California to set up in business. I remember hearing some about him when I was out in the gold fields back in '50 and '51. They said he was one of them who captured that outlaw Juaquin Murieta and cut off his head for to collect the bounty.

"When this war between the states started up, he got the itch to do some fighting but couldn't get a commission to suit him. So he got up this army of volunteers and offered to take them

East and fight. Instead, they got orders to stay out West and guard the roads and they ain't none too happy about it."

"But still, why not stay at the fort they're building in Nevada Territory?"

"I don't know if it's his own notion or if someone hinted he ought to do it, but the colonel thinks he's supposed to keep an eye on us Mormons right along with watchin' over the Paiutes and the Shoshonis."

This prompted a chorus of murmuring and mumbling among the men, but it was Brigham who voiced the question.

"Why? By God, I have informed Abe Lincoln and General Halleck and everyone else I thought might be interested that we are strong for the Constitution and have no intention of throwing in with the secessionists."

"True enough, as far as it goes. Some say—the colonel among them—it don't go far enough, since you've also said you want no part of their war. Not throwin' in with the secessionists ain't the same as siding with the Union."

"So what?" Brigham thundered. "What the hell do they care if we choose to sit by and watch them ruin the nation, rather than help them do it? They are only reaping what they've sowed with all their corruption!"

"Don't ask me. Ain't no need to yell at me, either. I'm just saying what's been said. They ain't no ideas of mine."

"You're right, Port. Of course. You have my apology. But, as you know, it don't take much to ruffle my feathers these days where the United States are concerned. Go ahead on."

He did. But what Rockwell had to say next did not sit any better with Brother Brigham and his minions.

"A couple of weeks ago, a red-headed man with side whiskers and mustache got off the eastbound mail coach here in the city. Maybe some of you seen him. He spent several days being sported around town by Governor Doty and other *federales*.

That was Colonel Patrick Connor. He wasn't in uniform, because he didn't want no one to know who he was or what he was up to. What he was up to was finding a place to put up a fort."

"Surely they will rebuild Camp Floyd, or Fort Crittenden, or whatever the hell they call it these days," Brigham Young said. "It was good enough for the army the last time they graced us with their presence. It ought to serve as well for this invasion of our sovereign soil."

"No, Brig, that ain't what he's planning a-tall. See, this Connor fellow either ain't as stupid as Albert Sydney Johnston was, or else he ain't as concerned about keeping the peace. He saw right off that Cedar Valley was good for nothing but cow pasture and that forty miles was too far from Salt Lake City should he have to put down a rebellion or some such."

"So, what are his intentions?"

"One day soon, Brig, you'll walk out your front door and look up Brigham Street and see Old Glory waving from the colonel's new flagpole."

"What are you saying?"

"He's going to build his camp right up there on the east bench at the mouth of Red Butte Canyon."

The earlier hubbub could not compare with the outburst this statement of Rockwell's prompted. Apostles were on their feet poking fingers in each other's chests, shaking fists in the air, and spewing profanity unbecoming in the mouths of the Lord's anointed.

But when all was said and done, Colonel Connor would build his camp right where he intended. And, to add insult to injury, he christened it Camp Douglas in honor of the late Stephen A. Douglas, who had been an enemy to the Mormons during their sojourn in his home state of Illinois, calling the Saints a "pestiferous, disgusting cancer."

Then, to add further insult, Connor permanently mounted a west-facing cannon at the camp, its barrel aimed menacingly at the estate of Brigham Young. Never mind that a shot from the cannon would fall far short of its target. The symbolism behind the threat was enough to satisfy Colonel Patrick Edward Connor and aggravate President Brigham Young.

CHAPTER FOUR

October 1862

Major Edward McGarry was experiencing some discomfort. He was not aware of its source, but its location was painfully obvious. It felt as if someone, a very strong man, was pressing the ball of his thumb into his left kidney. He shifted his hips about, attempting to dislodge whatever the troublesome object was. But the movement offered no relief and served only to push the major another step toward wakefulness.

Someone must be shining a lantern in my face, he thought, squeezing his eyes tighter shut in protest. Slowly, his mind awakened into a fuzzy semi-awareness. The next thing to penetrate that awareness was a terrible thirst. He worked his tongue around and screwed his lips about and learned that his mouth was sticky and foul. He wondered what someone might have fed him that tasted so rank.

Eventually—he knew not how long, for he had no sense of the passage of time as yet—McGarry cracked his left eyelid, using all his strength and concentration to keep the gap as narrow as possible. There was, in fact, an intense light shining on him. It was the sun. He lay as still as possible, examining the hazy scene before him as it filtered through his clenched eyelashes. He made out the shadow—silhouette, rather, he decided—of some fearsome beast. But it soon materialized into the head of a horse, bobbing from time to time and blocking the worst of the sun's rays. He wished it would stay still and leave the shade in place.

More of the world came into focus. Standing next to the horse was a man. As McGarry shifted his head a bit and invited his right eye to join the left, he became aware of several men standing nearby, each holding an impatient horse.

Soon, sounds penetrated his consciousness and started to take shape, if not make sense. The infernal buzz of some insect, almost inside his head. The snort of a blowing horse. A hack and a spit and the splattering gob. A hoof pawing the dirt. A sneeze. And that damned fly.

What the hell is going on here, he wondered. *Where am I? Who are these people? What have they done to me? What are they going to do to me?*

McGarry allowed his eyes to close again, lost in sensory overload. Then, like a blacksmith's hammer, it hit him. Cavalry patrol. Indians. He was in command. He rolled off the small rock under his back and onto his belly, pushed himself upright with tingly arms, rubbed his face briskly with the palms of his hands, focused bleary and burning eyes on the nearest man.

"What the hell's going on here?"

"Sir?"

"Don't be daft, you damn fool. What is your name?"

"Briggs, sir. John Briggs."

"Why are you standing there holding your horse, Briggs?"

"Orders, sir."

"Whose orders?"

"Yours, sir."

What the hell, McGarry wondered, *is this fool talking about?*

"You, over there! Captain Smith, isn't it?"

"Yessir."

"Come over here!"

The captain followed along as McGarry walked a short

distance from the assembled men, then turned to face him.

"Suppose you tell me what the hell's going on here, Captain. Why are all these men standing in the road holding their horses?"

It took Smith a second to recover from the blast of McGarry's breath before he could answer. "Well, sir, last evening you became upset at the men when you heard some grumbling about being assigned to this place and sent on this patrol. Nothing unusual, sir—just the usual sort of grousing.

"But you called us a bunch of goldbricks and slackers. And some other things I shan't repeat. Ordered us to dismount and lie down in the road and go to sleep. Said you would go off and fight the Indians by yourself."

"Did I include you in this criticism, Captain Smith?"

"It seemed so at the time, sir."

McGarry attempted to sort out what he had been told.

"Then why was I the one sleeping on the road?"

"After a few minutes you came back and cussed us some more. You ordered us to mount up, then to dismount and hold our horses. Then you laid down and went to sleep."

McGarry took off his hat and wiped a sleeve across his forehead, mopping away the sweat already beading up in the early morning sun. He studied the troopers and shook his head. "You mean to tell me that you and all these men have been standing here all night holding your horses?"

"Yessir."

"Did I seem all right to you when I issued those orders, Smith?"

"Not exactly, sir. We thought maybe someone had put something into your canteen without your knowing it, sir."

"And yet you obeyed my orders? And saw to it that these other men did, too?"

"Yessir."

The major's face flushed, the tinge creeping up from under his collar until clouding his cheeks a hue to match his already reddened nose. "But why, you blithering idiot? And don't give me any of that 'orders is orders' bullshit. I want the truth of it!"

Smith's face paled. His jaw worked in an attempt to assemble words. "Well, Major McGarry, sir, you, uh, you threatened to shoot anyone who disobeyed. Held a cocked revolver to Private Farley's head, you did. We thought you meant it, sir."

Major Edward McGarry was nothing if not a man of action. So, despite his inability to come to terms with what he had heard, he told the captain to have the men mount up, and they would resume patrol.

Maybe, he thought, if they could flush out a few Indians, and he could get a little killing done, this damn headache would go away.

Chapter Five

McGarry sat his horse, silently staring at the slow, almost stagnant stream. It could not be more than two feet deep at its deepest or thirty yards wide at its widest where it spread thin at the ford. The water was so milky that even in the shallows you could not see the riverbed through it.

He found it astounding that this place was a major crossing on the most important river on the busiest road in the far West: Gravelly Ford on the Humboldt River on the California Trail. Other than ruts left behind by thousands of wagons that rolled through here over the past fifteen years, McGarry saw no sign of life as far as he could see—which was a considerable distance in this country.

Nor could he see any sign of death.

But death had been here. Or so he had been told. In mid-September, the recently arrived California Volunteers at Fort Ruby were informed that the Shoshoni had murdered twenty-three emigrants at this place.

Colonel Patrick Connor dispatched Major Edward McGarry and a cavalry detail with orders to track down the offending Indians and "immediately hang them and leave their bodies thus exposed as an example of what evil-doers may expect while I command this district."

Connor left it up to McGarry to determine guilt but urged him to "destroy every male Indian whom you may encounter in the vicinity of the late massacres."

And now, here sat McGarry and two companies of cavalry. After more than two weeks later, the patrol had not hanged, shot, or even seen a single Indian.

But presently, by sheer happenstance, three Shoshoni men happened by. Curiosity got the better of them, and they were enticed into the soldier camp. When they later decided to leave, they were deemed escaping prisoners and shot and wounded by the guards. McGarry decided to finish the job rather than chance another escape. He ordered them shot dead.

Still, he was not content.

"Captain Smith!" McGarry called out that evening from where he stood at the tent flap of his field headquarters.

The captain came running and snapped to attention with a salute. "Sir!"

"Come in, please, Captain Smith."

"Yessir."

McGarry plopped down on a camp chair and stared up at the captain, standing at attention just inside the tent door. "At ease." He removed his hat and sailed it across the tent, where it spun to a stop atop the taut blanket on his cot. "Well, Smith, the men have their first taste of Indian killing. How does it sit with them?"

"Not well, sir. They had hoped for some fighting." Smith swallowed hard. "Shooting hostages isn't much to their taste."

"We'll see what we can do to remedy that, Captain. Saddle up at dawn and take your company and scout upriver for hostiles. I've a feeling they are in the vicinity. Bring them back if you can. Kill the bastards if they offer any resistance. Hang them. Shoot them. Just make damn sure they are dead, and leave the sonsabitches for the coyotes and crows."

"Am I to make any attempt to link them to wagon train killings, sir?"

"Don't bother. If there were any such killings, I see no sign

36

of it. The report is a mystery. In any event, the colonel's orders are explicit. And, even if the Indians did not kill anybody here, they have probably killed other travelers elsewhere. And will do so again. If not in retaliation, we will eliminate any of the damn savages we root out for purposes of prevention."

McGarry raked his fingers through lank hair. "Good luck, Captain. Dismissed." As the tent flap waved shut and Smith's footsteps faded, the major reached into a pack beside his chair, pulled out a flask, and swallowed a long draught of whiskey.

Smith and his troopers followed the Humboldt for miles hunting Indian sign. The lazy, alkali-soaked stream meandered through flatland and around skirted hillsides, its banks as often barren as lined with willows. Dust-covered sagebrush, shadscale, salt grass, greasewood, rabbitbrush, and rice grass scattered across a monotonous landscape in monochromatic shades of dun. Scrawny, contorted cedar trees peppered the north slopes of broken ridges and hills.

How the Shoshoni and Paiute scrounged a living out of this boundless desert was a wonder to Smith and the soldiers—and every other person not native to the land who passed this way. A shout from one of the troopers interrupted his reverie.

"Captain!"

Smith, startled, yanked back on the reins, the unexpected stop causing the horse to toss its head, rattling bit chains, and skirt backward a few steps. "What is it?"

"Look over there! Yonderway!"

He followed the outstretched arm and pointed finger of the trooper. There, on the same side of the river but separated twice by the stream owing to the bow of a meander, was a cluster of Indians. The band looked to be a mix of men and women. Some sat and kneeled over *metates*, the *manos* in their hands still as they stared back at the mounted soldiers. Others stood, likewise enthralled.

Smith surmised the Indians knew of their coming before the soldiers were aware of them, as the men held weapons—a couple had rifles; most carried short bows, some with spears. Knives and clubs dangled from waistbands. But, while alert, the Indians did not look to be hostile—no arrows nocked, rifles at rest, spears butted to the ground.

"Shall I order an attack, sir?"

Smith stared at the young officer. "No, Lieutenant. I sense no immediate threat from these Indians."

"But, sir! The major said—"

"I know what Major McGarry said, Lieutenant. We will punish these savages. But not here. Not now. Round them up. We will return to camp and question them there."

The troopers lined out and rounded the oxbow at a trot, fencing off the Indians, leaving the river as the only means of escape. A small contingent of mounted soldiers, dismounted with rifles in hand, remained across the bend to prevent a breakout.

The Indians, relieved of their arms, left behind what worldly goods they carried, to be driven like so many cattle to the cavalry camp at Gravelly Ford. Frightened and uncertain, the captives moved along without incident until passing, at the outskirts of the camp, the bloated, spoiling corpses of their companions.

The agitated Indians stirred like disturbed ants, frantic conversation and fearful shouting cutting the desert air. Anticipating trouble, Major McGarry ordered the soldiers in camp to arm themselves, and commanded Smith's mounted troopers to encircle the captives and kill any that attempted to break out.

The order went unfulfilled, as the Indians, sensing their fate, bolted for the river.

Splash turned to spray turned to mist as moccasined feet, steel-shod hooves, and leather boots roiled the shallow stream. Powder smoke fogged the slaughter, the roar of rifle and pistol punctuating the screams and choking of dying Indians.

Nine were killed in the escape attempt, their blood swirling and eddying in the slow waters of Gravelly Ford even as their corpses joined the others in a growing, smelly heap.

But McGarry was not finished, and patrols continued.

Six more prisoners came in under the guns of the troopers. Whether the major's mood took a turn for the better given the killing thus far accomplished, or whether he hoped to run up the score by luring in more candidates, cannot be known. In any event, in the long shadows of a rising sun, he sent two of the captive men away, with orders to return by nightfall with the Indians who had slaughtered the supposed occupants of the alleged wagon train.

Should they not return, McGarry said, he would execute the four braves left behind.

They did not, and he did.

The slaughter left three Shoshoni women still in the camp, survivors of the attempted escape. These, too, he released with a message for their band: if they did not leave the emigrants be, he would return next summer and destroy them all.

Even as they broke camp and started back to Fort Ruby, the soldiers got a head start on the summer's promise—eight more Shoshoni encountered and killed along the way.

McGarry's official report of the expedition noted but one regret: that they had been obliged to shoot rather than hang the Shoshoni as ordered, as he had been unable to locate any trees suitable for fulfilling Colonel Connor's command. Still, twenty-four dead Indians was twenty-four dead Indians.

Personally, he thought it a sorry payment on the outstanding debt of twenty-three dead emigrants. If there were any dead emigrants. But that did not concern him overmuch.

CHAPTER SIX

Frost came early high in the desert mountains. By the white-man month of October, the ever-endless tides of Shoshoni life carried the bands west, where pinyon pine trees carpeted the dusty, dry slopes of the Grouse Creek Mountains, the Pequops, the Rubys.

Bear Hunter's people, the followers of Sagwitch, and families who usually camped with Pocatello gathered and scattered across the mountain slopes where cedar and pinyon found root in the dry, rocky soil.

This time of harvest was at once a lazy one and a busy one. In the bracing morning air, small bands of The People spread out through the hills with sticks and bags and blankets in hand to relieve the pinyons of their heavy loads of pinyon cones fat with nuts and ripe for the taking after the first hard freeze. The tight green cones rained slowly down on blankets spread beneath the trees, detached from limbs and branches by a blow from a stick, the drag of a makeshift rake, the grasp of fingers sticky with pine gum that would turn dark and stain hands for weeks to come; no amount of scrubbing with sand or water would remove the blotches.

Everyone worked. The men tramped the hills trailing deer, rabbits, and other opportunities to make meat. Women and children harvested the pine cones and ferried the loads back to camp, stockpiling work for the late afternoon and evening. Old people tended camp, keeping stewpots bubbling over fires fragrant with burning cedar, pinyon, and sagebrush.

Chill mornings became warm days that turned uncomfortably hot as the sun hung in the sky, and the people shed layer after layer of clothing, recapitulating a year's wardrobe in the length of a day, only to wrap up again as the sun hung low, and its warmth fell out of the sky to disappear into the dirt and rocks, where it would cool to frost through the course of the night.

Campsites wandered from slope to slope high above the wide open and empty desert valleys of this basin and range country, and little that happened there escaped the notice of the Shoshoni. News spread from band to band to band with less speed but broader coverage than the white man's telegraph wire that stretched insignificantly across the deserts below.

As they sat around the fires in fading daylight coaxing winter food from the day's gathering of pine cones, The People exchanged information. Visitors wandered from one camp to another, helping with the work, sharing a meal, trading goods, telling stories, and reporting news. Neighboring was as much a part of the fall ritual as extracting pinyon nuts.

Spread on flat stones and tucked into low flames or atop glowing embers, the pine cones warmed and dried as the travelers did likewise at this night's camp. Slowly, ever so slowly, the thick scales on the pine cones released their grip and peeked open. Likewise, the bearers of news made small talk, telling of minor happenings among others of The People lately visited, eventually loosening up and opening the way for stories of more importance.

Laid out on blankets, the pine cones, no longer green and sticky and tight, but dry and brown and brittle from the heat of the fires, were flailed with limber sticks to release the bounty within. Scales shattered and broke free, spitting out savory nuts.

Tossed into the fires, empty cones exhaled the perfume of burning sap.

This evening, hanging in the air with the smoke and sweet scent, was news bitter and foul.

"Soldiers have come. From the west," a man from Pocatello's band said.

Bear Hunter mulled that over for a time. "There have been soldiers in the west for some time. We know they built Fort Churchill over there a couple of years ago when they were fighting the Paiutes."

"These soldiers are different. They came from over the mountains in California and stopped only briefly at Fort Churchill, then marched on."

Sagwitch said, "How many are they?"

"Many. Nearly a thousand I would say."

"Where are they going?"

"They have stopped for now near that mail and stage station in Ruby Valley. They are building a fort."

Bear Hunter scoffed. "A fort! There? There is nothing there! That place is good only for watering horses and hunting ducks."

"Nevertheless, it is true. I have heard they chose that place because it is halfway along the road from Carson City to Salt Lake City. From Ruby Valley, they think they can protect the Overland Trail through the desert and the emigrant trail along the Humboldt."

"How foolish," Bear Hunter said. "They will freeze and starve this winter. Besides, by the time they saddle their lazy American horses any Indians they are foolish enough to chase after will be long gone."

"These soldiers have already killed some of The People. Over at the Humboldt crossing they call Gravelly Ford they killed two dozen. Some they shot trying to run away, some because they did not want to go with the soldiers, some just because

43

they were of The People."

"But why? What did the soldiers want in the first place?" Sagwitch said.

"They were looking for some Indians they said killed some white travelers at that place. But none of those captured or killed by the soldiers had anything to do with that. I have heard there weren't even any whites killed—that it was all a story someone made up."

Sagwitch wrapped his robe higher around his shoulders and hunkered lower on his backrest. "This is troubling news, these soldiers. But as long as they stay in Ruby Valley, I do not think they will bother us. It is a long way from their fort to our valleys."

"Then this next news will trouble you even more, Sagwitch. And you, Bear Hunter. Only some of the soldiers are staying in Ruby Valley. Most of them are moving on. They are already packing up, in fact."

"Where are they going?" the leaders asked, as if with one voice.

"I do not know for sure. But I know they are going to where the Mormons live."

Sagwitch said, "That is good. I have dealt with those Mormons many times. They do not like the American soldiers. When the bluecoats came before, that Mormon big man, Brigham Young, talked with them, and they left us alone. Maybe he will do the same again."

Pulling his blanket tighter around his shoulders, Sagwitch cracked open a pine nut with his teeth and peeled off the brittle shell. He savored the sweet meat as he thought. Then, "I will talk to my Mormon friends in Willow Valley. They will know what to do."

The man from Pocatello's people and Sagwitch stood and shook the dust and debris from their blankets. As they walked away to the fires in their own camp circles, Bear Hunter stared into the dying fire. He lifted his eyes to look across the broad valley that lay below the campsite on the mountain ridge and saw only emptiness disappearing into the falling darkness.

CHAPTER SEVEN

The jumble of rocks thereabouts had sat still and unmoving forever. The dirt moved only when sprouting grass or wandering greasewood roots pushed it aside.

Even the cedar trees were still. Unlike their cousins, the aspens in the mountains and canyons that seemed always to shiver, these cedars stirred only in a stiff breeze and, even then, barely whispered.

So quiet was this place that Bear Hunter could have closed his eyes and imagined himself the only living thing on the earth, the intake and exhalation of his breath the only motion. The illusion was spoiled only by the scent of sagebrush and juniper berries that hung like curtains in the calm desert air.

In such a place, Bear Hunter thought, sitting as still as the stones around him for a few hours should be a manageable task. He had left the harvest camps in the mountains to the north for this place beside the Overland Trail to satisfy himself that the stories about the soldiers were true, and to see for himself the size and strength of this army invading the land of The People.

For reasons he could not explain even to himself, this was a thing he wanted to do himself. He could have sent a scout from his band. Had he done so, he would have cautioned the man not to get this close to the trail, to stay well away and observe from a safe distance.

But Bear Hunter did not follow that advice. From the place

he had chosen for his reconnaissance, he could easily shoot an arrow into the heart of anyone passing on the road below. Much as he believed that he could absorb stillness and silence from the surrounding stones, he held the opinion that, by staring into the soldiers' eyes, taking in their odors, hearing their voices, he could absorb knowledge of their intentions.

This place was in the territory of the Gosiute people, who somehow eked a living out of this harsh land. The chief much preferred the richer lands along the *Boa Ogoi,* the Big River, where his people lived. Even the lands to the north and west of this place where other Shoshoni bands lived, while harsher than his own country, were preferable to these alkali deserts and mountains of broken stone.

From his vantage point, he could see endlessly across sand dunes and alkali flats to the north as well as seeing great distances across the miles to the east and south, where the grass- and brush-covered plains rose into rough mountains— the Dugways, the Thomas Range, the Drums, the Little Drums, the House Range, as the white men called them.

The soldiers on the Overland Trail would come to this place from directly behind Bear Hunter, from the opposite side of the mountain ridge on which he sat. A half dozen miles west of him, the eastbound road hit the slope of the Fish Creek Mountains and veered sharply north to loop around the end of the range before turning south to pass his position, after which the road again resumed its eastbound course.

He knew the column must pass here, as the road was pinched into a narrow place between the steep slope where he sat and the network of ponds and marshes called Fish Springs, whose reeds and rushes carpeted a few square miles of the desert like a misplaced, cast-aside robe.

Before he heard or saw any evidence of the approaching army, Bear Hunter smelled them coming. Even his weak old nose detected the dust raised by the soldiers, drifting invisibly in the desert air. Then, from the north came the soldier scouts, lazing along in their saddles and paying no attention to the world around them. Certainly, they expected no trouble in this place.

A few minutes later, cavalry columns rounded the point and plodded into view. Even though many of the troopers seemed to Bear Hunter to ride in their sleep, the horses still traveled in strict rows of four with precise gaps separating their arcane divisions and subdivisions. No matter how often he saw traveling cavalry columns, their disciplined order of march never failed to amuse the old chief.

Row after row after row of horses and riders shuffled by for many minutes. After a suitable interval, the cavalry and the dragoons were followed up by repeated ranks of infantry tramping lazily along the road. There were so many soldiers—more than eight hundred, by his count—that Bear Hunter could not imagine they had left some behind at Fort Ruby.

And still the army came.

After the troops, wagons. More than fifty of them, he guessed. A few fancy carriages carrying officers and the women and children who must be their families, some in enclosed wagons they called ambulances, and a long, long train of supply wagons.

But even that was not the end.

Trudging along the road through dust by then ground fine as flour and cut deeper than their hooves came hundreds of cattle. All those supply wagons and that herd could feed The People for a good long time, Bear Hunter thought as he watched bovine backsides disappear in the distance ahead of the receding shouts and whistles of soldier cowboys.

There is something different about these soldiers, Bear Hunter thought. While he could not put his finger on it, there was something foreboding, something threatening, in this army. Dread lingered in the air with the dust. *This time, Sagwitch may be wrong. I do not believe these soldiers will listen to the Mormons. Their ears will not hear.*

Once the dust settled and he was satisfied there were no stragglers to discover his presence, Bear Hunter rose from his seat among the boulders and started the two-mile hike to the place he had concealed his horses. It would take several days' riding to intercept his band as they made their way slowly back to the *Boa Ogoi* country.

Plenty of time to contemplate what the arrival of these soldiers meant for his people.

CHAPTER EIGHT

The hat in his hands turned slowly round and round, and his boot heel tapped incessantly as Porter Rockwell sat in Brigham Young's outer office in the Beehive House. From time to time he heard muffled voices and rustling behind the closed door that led to the inner sanctum.

The knob turned, and the door opened a bit. "President Young will see you now, Brother Rockwell," said the man who poked his head out through the door he held partly closed.

"Thank you, George. It's about damn time."

When Rockwell stood, the secretary retracted his head, then, a few seconds later, swung the door wide. A door on the adjacent wall, leading elsewhere in the big house, latched shut as Rockwell entered the room. His leader sat in an overstuffed chair next to a rolltop desk.

The secretary indicated a side chair for the visitor, then took his own seat in a wheeled chair at the desk and took up a pen.

"No record of this meeting will be required, Brother Watt."

"Am I excused, then, Brother Brigham?"

"No. Stay, please. You can serve as my extra set of ears—and an aid to my memory, if you will."

Young turned to his guest. "Tell me what you have learned, Port. And be quick about it. I've much business to attend to."

Rockwell looked up from his hat, still rotating in his hands, and cleared his throat. "It's like this. The soldiers is for certain on the way and will likely be here in a week's time, if they don't

50

dawdle. They ain't in no particular hurry, but they're on the way."

"Any change to the reports that they intend to build their fort here in the city?"

"I haven't heard such."

"So, they won't be stopping at Fort Crittenden?"

Rockwell laughed. "Well, they'll stop for a bit, anyways."

"What are you saying?"

"You know that big flagpole—'bout the only thing they left out there? Me and some of the boys, we cut it down."

"So? I know that. I as much as ordered it."

"Well, we left it laying in the road. That army'll have to stop long enough to move it."

The corners of Young's mouth darted upward but immediately returned to their accustomed tight-lipped, downward-turned bow. "That will not take but a minute. What I want to know is, what more have you learned of their intentions?"

Connor, Rockwell said, intended to cross the bridge across the Jordan River, some eight miles south and a bit west of the center of the city. From there, rather than taking the most direct route to the site east of the city where he intended to build his fort, he would march up East Temple Street to the center of the city and stop at the governor's mansion—near Young's residence and the headquarters of all things Mormon—before proceeding to the east bench and pitching his tent.

The bow of Brigham Young's mouth turned further downward. A furrow between his eyebrows deepened. He shifted his bulk in the chair and grasped the lapels of his jacket, then shifted his grip to the arms of the chair, knuckles whitening in the clench. "Why is he doing this? What is he up to?"

Rockwell studied his leader for a time before answering. "I think you know, Brig. He ain't no different from them that has been kickin' us around since Joseph started this outfit. That sonofabitch has got a uniform, and he's got an army, and I suspect he'll use 'em both to make life hell for us."

Young nodded. "I suspect so. What can we do to stop him?"

"Nothin' much. Leastways not right off. Some of the boys is sayin' we should stop them at the bridge and not allow the bastards to cross the river. Some are ridin' through town offering five-hundred-dollar bets that the army won't cross the Jordan. They ain't got no takers, from what I'm told."

"Can it be done? Can they be stopped?"

"I'd have to say no. Hell, they've got soldiers and supplies spread out for miles on the trail. Even if we was to pull down the bridge, they've got the means to put up a new one, else find another way across and ride right through whatever resistance we could put up. Oh, we could lay waste to a lot of 'em, all right. Leastways for a while. But they've got us outgunned."

Young drummed his fingertips on the arm of the chair. He pursed his lips and furrowed his brow and clenched his jaws. Sweat beaded on his forehead and upper lip. George Watt handed him a handkerchief. At last, "We will bide our time. Sooner or later, Connor will make a mistake. We will be ready."

You have to understand the Mormons—the Church of Jesus Christ of Latter-day Saints. And, once you do, you will understand how they came to be in this isolated place at that time in the deserts of the far West. And why the Americans hated them so. And why the Saints returned that sentiment with such passion.

It is a religion that sprang forth in the eighteen-twenties from the fecund ground of the Finger Lakes region of New York State, where spiritual revivals, faith healing, heavenly manifestations, and folk magic held sway. There, the boy Joseph Smith had been visited by Jesus Christ and God the Father themselves who informed him that he had been chosen to restore the fullness of the Gospel upon the earth. A series of angels kept the lad in contact with the heavens and led him to a stack of gold plates engraved in an antique language from which he translated the *Book of Mormon.* He then returned the original documents to the angels.

The book tells tales of bands of Israelites who abandoned the Holy Land at various junctures in its ancient depravity to colonize the new world and live the Christian life. But they fought among themselves and the last honest man among them was murdered by his wicked cousins, whose blood now flowed in the veins of the American Indians. And even though they were a fallen people, the Mormons believed that Israelite blood granted the Indians a special place in God's plan, and it was their charge to redeem them.

The Mormons were repulsive to their neighbors for a variety of reasons, not least among them the unshakable belief that they were the chosen people and thus entitled to look down their noses at the gentiles. But there was more.

Where Americans were fiercely competitive and individualistic, Mormons were cooperative and communitarian. Where Americans held to one man, one vote, the Mormons cast their ballots in blocks so their political influence outweighed their numbers. Where Americans valued religion as a part of life largely separate from politics, Mormons saw their church and government as inseparable to the point that they fully expected the nation to disintegrate at any moment, at which time their elders would pick up the pieces and use them to fashion the Kingdom of God on earth.

And then there was celestial marriage—plural marriage—polygamy.

The Mormons believed this doctrine of multiple wives was but one of many that had been, and more that would be, restored from Old Testament times. Church members embraced the principle with equal parts glee and repugnance. Americans could not countenance the practice and considered it nothing more than lusty whoremongering.

So, the Mormons had been kicked out of every place they congregated in the States, from New York to Ohio to Missouri to Illinois. They escaped the nation in an exodus of biblical proportions to the West, to settle in the mountains and valleys of the Great Basin where Mexico claimed ownership but exercised no control.

But no sooner had the Mormons unpacked the wagons than the Mexican War once again placed them squarely within the borders of the United States of America. Still, isolated in an unwanted promised land of deserts and canyons, they set out to establish Zion, the Kingdom of God, the independent State of Deseret, without concern for the government that had refused to protect them from, and even cooperated in, their mistreatment—the expulsions, the thievery, the mobbery, the murder.

The Saints quickly spread far and wide across the land, with the settlements of Deseret stretched thin from the Salmon River in the north to San Bernardino in the south, and from the backside of the Wasatch Mountains to the Sierra Nevada range. Here, they happily went about their business governed in all things—religious, political, economic—by the priesthood of the Church of Jesus Christ of Latter-day Saints.

But in a growing nation hell-bent on Manifest Destiny, no place stays isolated for long, and the Saints were soon overrun by gold rushers and emigrants, whose lines of supply and communication to the more heavily populated reaches of the United States passed through the heart of Zion.

The Americans were still suspicious of these Mormons. And now, the curious attitude of the Saints toward Indians came into play. In their belief that the Indians were among the Lord's elect, and that emancipating them from the depravity of their fallen state was a command from on high, the Mormons sought to ally with the tribes. Such doctrines had caused concern years ago in Missouri but had attained a higher place on the hierarchy of reasons to fear the Mormons since their move west. The possibility, however vague, of an alliance between the Saints and the western tribes amounted to an enemy that politicians east and west did not care to contemplate.

You will recall the history the Mormons assigned to the American Indians: descent from wandering Israelites of the ancient world. Thus, the Indians were kin and deserving—upon repentance—of a favored place in the religious order of the eternities. The Mormons even had a moniker for them: "Lamanites," a label derived from the name of a disobedient son of an obedient hero in the *Book of Mormon.*

All of this meant the Mormons were not willing to merely kick the Indians aside and kill them if they refused to move. At least as a first resort. It was the plan of the prophet Brigham Young to embrace the tribal people as brothers, to welcome them into the fold, to share the land and its resources, to live in peace and harmony in Zion while they all awaited the imminent return of Jesus Christ. His teaching from the pulpit was that it was cheaper to feed the Indians than fight them.

Such attitudes, of course, were wholly un-American. So, the Mormons were accused of conspiring with the Shoshoni, the Paiutes, the Gosiutes, the Utes, and all their branches to make war upon the United States of America. The Saints were charged with the direction of, participation in, or involvement with every attack on every wagon train, every theft, every murder, every kidnapping between South Pass and Donner Summit, from the Snake River to San Diego.

The suspicions were not altogether without merit. Witness the Mountain Meadows Massacre. Even Brigham Young himself on occasion referred to his Lamanite brethren as "the battle-ax

of the Lord."
And into this fraught situation rode the California Volunteers.

CHAPTER NINE

December 1862

Whiskey, if not watered too thin, was, to McGarry's way of thinking, the best defense against cold. Unlike clothing or sunshine or fire, alcohol warmed from the inside out and worked its way deep down into the bones. The major, filled with such warmth, was not particularly bothered by the chill in the air the fourth night of December on the road north from Salt Lake City.

He could not vouch for the comfort of the one hundred cavalry troops accompanying him. The army provided a small ration of alcohol on such marches, but the amount was so paltry as to be practically useless. Colonel Connor was a stickler about such things, allowing only the prescribed portion and not a drop more. Even so, McGarry habitually added, from his own stores, many times the amount allowed for personal use. And he did not doubt that others among the troops used his same method of warding off the cold. So long as the men were able to stay mounted, McGarry did not care. Besides, Connor was not along on this expedition, and he could not be hurt by what he did not know. Nor could McGarry and the troopers in his command.

The night had been a long one. They were bound for Empey's Ferry on the Bear River, a ride of some seventy or eighty miles from Camp Douglas. Connor had dispatched the troops late in the day, so the greater part of the ride had occurred under cover of darkness, minimizing the chance of discovery by the Shoshoni. Their mission, their orders, were to recover livestock stolen from emigrants that the Indians were said to be holding somewhere near the ferry. The soldiers were to root them out, recover the stolen animals, and brook no nonsense from the Indians in the doing.

Although he detested the fatigue and discomfort that accompanied night travel in winter, McGarry would rather be on the way to an Indian fight than hanging around the camp overseeing the digging of dugouts or the construction of log foundations upon which tents were fixed. Such were the quarters at Camp Douglas at present; only Colonel Connor was afforded the luxury of a permanent structure, which served as both office and home. But, even if he had had a palace for his billet, McGarry would still prefer hunting Indians to camp duty.

As long, that is, as he could stay warm.

McGarry had barely caught his breath from a previous expedition before being dispatched by Connor for this one. It had been but a little more than a week ago that he had ridden back to Salt Lake City, having rescued the supposed Van Ornum boy from Bear Hunter's band in Cache Valley. While less than pleased at being sent out on what he saw as a personal errand for that demanding sonofabitch Zachias Van Ornum, he had willingly accepted the assignment as preferable to serving as little more than a construction foreman at camp.

"Major McGarry," Connor had said upon summoning him to headquarters one November morning, "I have an assignment for you."

The other man in the room approached and offered a handshake. "I am Zachias Van Ornum, Major. I am pleased to make your acquaintance. Are you familiar with the Van Ornum name?"

McGarry allowed that he was not.

"It is a name familiar to many throughout the West. I will tell you why," Van Ornum said, and McGarry mentally settled in for a long story.

"No need, Mister Van Ornum," Connor said. "Allow me to lay out the essentials for the major."

Van Ornum nodded agreement, but McGarry sensed he was miffed at being denied the opportunity to tell his tale. He seemed the type who enjoyed hearing his own voice.

"Two years ago September, Mister Van Ornum's brother was with a train of wagons on the Oregon Trail along the Snake River north and west of here. At a place where Salmon Falls Creek joins the river, a band of renegade Shoshoni ambushed the train, then laid siege to it for a day or two before driving off the survivors and plundering the wagons and stealing all the stock.

"Them that got away were stranded in the desert and starving to death, waiting for help. Van Ornum and his family and some others opted to leave the rest and set off to make their own way. Which they did."

Connor looked to Van Ornum for verification. The visitor nodded his approval, then opened his mouth to speak. The colonel talked on, cutting off Van Ornum even before he started.

"Later on, a cavalry detail found what remained of them. The Indians had killed and mutilated most of the unfortunate emigrants, but the troopers determined Van Ornum's three daughters and a son were taken alive. The soldiers made every effort to rescue the children but were unsuccessful in tracking down the renegades that held them.

"Anyway, the savages did not hold the children long—at least the girls. The troopers learned later that they had starved to death. But the boy, they were told by Indian informants, was still alive. Since then, Mister Van Ornum here has attempted to find his nephew. He has tracked down reports of his whereabouts from hell to breakfast. He has learned lately that there's a white boy living with Bear Hunter's band up north in Cache Valley—what the savages call Willow Valley—and has reason to believe the boy is his nephew. Have I got it right, Mister Van Ornum?"

"Yes, Colonel, that's the gist of it," he told Connor, then turned his attention to McGarry. "I got word of the new military presence here in Salt Lake City and came hoping to convince Colonel Connor to mount a rescue expedition."

From all appearances you've been successful, thought McGarry. It was not like the colonel to pander to civilians, so McGarry was at a loss to understand why he would agree to risk the lives of soldiers and expend government resources for such a purpose. His curiosity was soon satisfied.

"I have had an increasing number of reports that the Shoshoni up north are growing bolder and more demanding and are becoming a grave danger to both settlers and travelers," Connor said. "While I care little for the fate of the treasonous Mormons living up there, we must demonstrate to the Indians that any difficulties they afford travelers will be met with swift reprisals.

"Rescuing the Van Ornum boy gives us a reasonable excuse for a show of force. Reports say the boy was seen with Bear Hunter's band, and they are said to be in Cache Valley. I have sent word that, if they do not release the boy, we will wipe out every one of them.

"Those, essentially, are your orders, Major McGarry. Am I clear?"

So, McGarry had followed Zachias Van Ornum to Cache Valley. He located Bear Hunter and his band near a small settlement called Providence and attacked without warning. Somehow, though, that damned old Indian had read his intentions and beat it into the mountains a few miles to the east, holding off the troopers from concealment in a small canyon.

When the chief came out under a white flag to parley, McGarry took him hostage. Later, he arranged to trade the old chief for the white boy.

The boy did not speak English and seemed to McGarry a Shoshoni in every respect save the blue eyes and blond hair hiding under layers of filth. They all but hogtied the boy to get him to come along.

Van Ornum, himself unsure of the boy's parentage, nevertheless declared the mission a success.

All told, McGarry thought, the entire episode had been a bust. The Indians insisted the boy was not the missing Van Ornum boy, but the son of a French trapper and a Shoshoni woman. McGarry suspected they were right.

Connor's intention of frightening the Shoshoni had likely failed as well, since the battle, such as it was, was a stalemate at best. Although they could not find any bodies, and the Shoshoni insisted none of their people had been killed, McGarry could not help but believe someone had died in the skirmish and so listed in his reports three Shoshoni killed.

"Major McGarry, sir."

McGarry was jolted back to the present by Captain Dan McLean. He looked around and noticed that dawn was upon them, although sunrise was yet a long time off, given their position at the western base of tall mountains.

"Yes, Captain?"

"The men sent out as scouts have returned, sir. Empey's Ferry is just ahead. The Shoshoni camp is visible a ways west of there. The ferry crosses the Bear River, and a mile or two beyond to the west is a smaller stream, the Malad River. They're camped on a rise just across it. For now."

"What the hell do you mean 'for now,' McLean?"

"It would appear they were warned of our coming. They have

cut the ferry rope and are breaking camp."

"Sonofabitch! Red bastards!" McGarry said, wondering how their presence had been betrayed. They rode on, and he warmed himself with several swigs from his canteen. They arrived at the ferry, and the rope had, indeed, been cut. The major turned up a scow belonging to Empey, the ferry operator, and the boat was used to row the troops across the Bear River, which was accomplished in several trips. The horses, by necessity, were left behind.

The unhorsed cavalry made its way up the bluffs separating the cut of the Bear from the Malad. The Shoshoni camp, mostly dismantled by now, was visible across the way. Not all the Shoshoni were cautious though; the troops managed to nab four men who were wandering between the rivers. McGarry sent a message to the Indian camp, demanding the stolen stock be gathered and delivered to him by noon, or the hostages would be killed.

His command was ignored. In fact, the Shoshoni's response was to show McGarry their backsides by lighting out on a trail to the north.

True to his word, McGarry killed the prisoners. And the means he chose for the killing was both dramatic and brutally cold blooded.

The troopers hauled in the cut ferry rope and used it to bind the Shoshoni men along its length like links in a chain. Not bothering to assemble a firing squad, McGarry invited any and all troopers with an inclination to do so to gun the men down. Fifty-one rounds later—or at some point during the fusillade— the Indians were dead.

The army unceremoniously dumped the bullet-riddled corpses into the river where, it must be assumed, they floated the twenty miles downstream to the Bear River Bay of the Great Salt Lake, there to be pickled in the brine.

CHAPTER TEN

The Shoshoni camp near Little Mountain, west of the Mormon village called Smithfield, was a pleasant one. Bear Hunter hoped to keep his village there until moving north to join Sagwitch and the families in his band at the winter camp at Beaver Creek.

The camp at Little Mountain had not been chosen for defensive purposes, and Bear Hunter, an experienced fighter, knew it was vulnerable to attack. And, more and more, he feared that attack would not be long in coming.

The latest fuel to fire his fears was heaped on by Terikee, a visitor to the camp from his home band across the divide. Terikee carried troubling news—if you could call it news, Bear Hunter thought, the story being someone's interpretation of what someone else supposedly heard from somebody. Still, it was a troublesome story and worth looking into.

Rumors were flying thick as mosquitoes over a summer marsh, it seemed.

The settlers were saying the Shoshoni said they intended to kill every white man who crossed the river.

The Shoshoni were saying the settlers in Box Elder said the Mormons in Cache Valley were going to kill every Indian that did not quit the country.

It was said the federal Indian agent, James Doty, would not distribute any more goods to the Shoshoni because he would seem to be rewarding killers.

It was said Brigham Young was abandoning his policy of feed-

63

ing the Indians, rather than fighting them, and laying plans to wage war.

It was said the Shoshoni planned to steal all the cows in Cache Valley and drive the herd north into the Salmon River country.

It was said . . .

Bear Hunter had heard enough rumors. He did not know what to believe. No one seemed to have direct knowledge of anything; everyone seemed to have heard something. So, he had summoned Sagwitch and asked him to talk to the Mormon leaders in Cache Valley and find out the truth of their intentions.

Sagwitch, more than any other leader of The People, had befriended and become a friend of the Mormons. He was always willing to give his friends the benefit of the doubt and automatically dismissed any suggestion of Mormon treachery.

Sagwitch was able to talk to the Mormons when no other Shoshoni could. And, while it was likely the settlers might misinform or mislead Sagwitch, and that Sagwitch might be inclined to believe them no matter what they said, Bear Hunter thought it preferable to listen to what the Mormons had to say instead of listening to more rumors.

And now Sagwitch was back. Soon, the other chiefs and elders would gather to hear his report. The young men, of course, would be there if only to cause contention.

Bear Hunter hoped Sagwitch would have good news. Although he was recognized as war chief over several bands of The People—including those of Lehi, Pocatello, and Sanpitch—Bear Hunter was not eager for war. Besides, every leader, every man for that matter, retained a degree of independence and could choose to go his own way regardless of Bear Hunter's leadership.

Bear Hunter feared that, should war come, it would be a long fight, and the People were in no condition to wage a protracted war. They lacked sufficient supplies of food. They lacked sufficient arms and were perpetually short of ammunition for those they had. While arrows shot from Shoshoni bows were lethal, arrows were no match for bullets.

And the Shoshoni were outnumbered. The settlers just kept coming, and the Mormons had countless brothers within a few days' ride who could come to their aid.

Then there was the troubling presence of the American soldiers, who had already demonstrated a penchant for cruelty and brutality, and a willingness to kill without asking questions.

In spite of it all, Bear Hunter wondered if his reluctance was a function of age. He was no longer a young man. As a matter of fact, he was old. Ancient, as far as some of the hot-blooded young warriors were concerned. Even Sagwitch, who was seeing his fortieth winter—an advanced age among the Shoshoni— seemed young to Bear Hunter.

Perhaps, Bear Hunter thought, I have lost my fighting spirit and should ask The People to choose a new war chief with more stomach for a fight. There were many among Pocatello's band always eager for a fight and others among Sanpitch's and Lehi's people who had grown tired of Mormon encroachment and were ready to resist.

But he would not do it. He would maintain his position as long as The People wanted him, and he would work against a fight with Sagwitch as his ally. Not so much because he feared fighting, he decided, but because he feared that if there were to be a fight it would be the last for his people.

"Here is what happened," Sagwitch said to the men gathered in council. "I went first to Israel Clark. He is a man some of you know. He leads the Mormon Minute Men, who are always chasing around after stolen horses. I asked him to ask his leader, Peter Maughan, if it is true that the Mormons are now enemies of The People—if they intend to fight us or to help the American soldiers fight us.

"Israel Clark talked to Peter Maughan, and then he came to find me. He said that Peter Maughan told him it was not true. That the Mormons are still our friends. And that Peter Maughan wanted me to come to Wellsville and talk to him in person.

"I rode down to that town with Israel Clark to see Peter Maughan. He took me into his house and gave me a meal. And then we talked. There were no other men there, but Peter Maughan is the head of the Mormons in Cache Valley and speaks for them all. But, as we know, in some ways the Mormons are like The People, and they do not always listen to their chiefs or do what they are supposed to do. Still, this is what Peter Maughan said.

"He said the Mormons are angry at their Shoshoni brothers. They give us food and food and more food, always more food, and some of their people complain that they go hungry to feed us. And we thank them by stealing their horses and their cattle, trampling their gardens and fields, frightening their women and children, and killing people on the roads and even some of the settlers."

"It is not true!" Chipmunk, one of the young men shouted. "We do not kill the settlers! And we shoot at them only if they are shooting at us!"

Sagwitch said, "That is true, most of the time. But we are not the only People, the only Shoshoni, and to the white men an Indian is an Indian. Besides, there have been times the only reason you ruffians didn't kill settlers is because you are so terrible at shooting. Remember the time you boasted that you shot the hat off that man? It is not because that is what you intended. He was lucky your aim is bad, or he would be dead. Others have not been so lucky."

"You take the Mormons' side instead of The People's!" another young man said.

"It is not a matter of one side or another," Bear Hunter said, hoping for calm. "We must hear what the Mormons are saying. Let Sagwitch talk."

"I tried to tell Peter Maughan that the reason we always need more food is because all our traditional foods have disappeared since they came here. The seeds and grasses and bulbs we harvest have been plowed under or trampled down by their cattle and sheep. The deer and elk have been driven away, and the fish in the streams are gone. If there is no food, we must take their cattle and horses or starve.

"I told Peter Maughan that The People let the white men come and live in our country. We welcomed the Mormons from the first day they came here. But, I told him, they are wearing out their welcome, because now too many of them have come.

"I asked him what we were supposed to eat if they destroyed our food and did not replace it. He did not know. He said the Mormons would give us as much as they could afford. But he warned that we must stop stealing their horses and cattle and harassing them in their villages."

"Enough of all this talk," Bear Hunter said, his patience worn thin. "What do you think, Sagwitch: are the Mormons our friends, or will they help the soldiers kill us?"

"I think it is up to us. Many of the Mormons do not like the American soldiers and do not want them here. But, if we keep bothering the Mormons, they won't want us here, either. Then they will ask the soldiers to fight us, and probably they will help them fight us."

CHAPTER ELEVEN

Something was disturbing the horse herd. Hoofbeats pounded the ground, and whinnies ripped through the darkness. As his mind struggled to find its bearings, he blinked his way out of deep sleep. Bear Hunter's first thoughts were of marauding wolves—but he had not seen wolves in this part of the country for years.

The old chief pulled on his leggings and then straightened his breechcloth as he ducked under the flap on his tipi. Already, several other men were up and about; he could just make them out in the dim glow from the stars in the sky, the only light in this, the dark of the moon.

The thundering hooves seemed to be drawing closer. And, Bear Hunter realized, they were from the wrong direction to be coming from their horse herd—these came from the opposite side of the camp. A horse trotted through the village, coming within a few yards of the chief. As it passed, its rider let loose a loud, falsetto scream of unbridled exuberance. Then horses were all around. Milling, snorting, pawing, frightened, sucking wind, dozens of horses hazed by mounted men came into and passed out of the village, their passage endangering The People who were out and about in the darkness before dawn.

By the time they were gone, Bear Hunter had sorted it out. The riders were young men from his band. The horses were stolen.

For weeks now, a handful of hot-blooded warriors, most of

them little more than boys, had rampaged throughout the Cache Valley, with an occasional foray through the gap cut by the *Boa Ogoi* into the lower Bear River Valley, stealing horses. More than a hundred mounts, by his count. And no amount of talking by him or the other chiefs could convince them that such behavior was folly.

Granted, horse stealing had a long tradition among The People, as it had among many tribes. It was good sport and great fun. But white men did not see the humor in it. In fact, these Mormons, including those who had settled in Cache Valley, were an altogether humorless lot. And Bear Hunter sensed they had just about had their fill of horse thieves, and that retaliation of one kind or another was in the offing.

Perhaps the Mormons would withhold the gifts—the payments—the bribes—of food The People had come to rely on since the coming of the Mormons had upset their ways of gathering food.

Only the wild berries and acorns and pinyon nuts remained reliable, as they grew on the mountainsides where the white man's plows could not reach. But those foods were but a portion of a complex and varied diet developed over the ages. The thick grasses that carpeted the valleys, from which they traditionally harvested edible seeds for food and flour, were now closely cropped by herds of cattle and thus rendered unproductive. The roots and stems they once gathered were now trampled under the hooves of cattle and horses. The streams were fished out. The deer and antelope and elk disappeared or were killed off. Small game and birds and ducks and geese were scarce, hunted more intensively by the white men than the Shoshoni ever had.

In recompense, the Mormons supplied Bear Hunter's bands with tons of wheat, both whole grain and ground into flour. Other cereal grains. Potatoes and vegetables. Bacon. And beef.

Butchered and on the hoof, entire herds of beef passed from Mormon hands into Shoshoni bellies.

But still, The People were hungry. And if, with all this horse stealing, the settlers opted to suspend or even eliminate the supplies as punishment, hunger could easily become starvation in the winter months to come.

Bear Hunter's village lay west of Smithfield at the southern end of Little Mountain near where Newton Creek poured into the Bear River, not far from where it plunged into the divide and left Cache Valley. Not a difficult place to find, if you were Mormon Minute Men in search of stolen horses.

And find it they did.

The morning sun was not long in the sky when armed settlers, fifty or sixty strong, rode out of its glare and into the camp.

One of the men, the one named Israel Clark who was head of the militia, said, "Bear Hunter, we've come for our horses."

"I do not have your horses."

"We don't want to waste time here. You Indians have stole more than a hundred horses lately."

"You will find no stolen horses here."

"Maybe yes, maybe no, Bear Hunter. But if you ain't hiding our horses, you're hiding them that took them. Like I said, we don't intend to waste time. We mean to get our horses back if it takes using these guns to do it."

These men mean business, Bear Hunter thought. He had heard the young men had divided the horses into several small herds and secreted them in as many out-of-the-way places. He did not think the thieves would give them all up, but perhaps if he could recover some of the horses, these men would be satisfied and leave them alone.

"Wait. I will see if anyone knows anything."

"We won't wait long."

Bear Hunter walked through the camp, summoning several men of the band as he went, including Sagwitch, the chief who knew the Mormons best. He felt fortunate the neighboring leader had chosen this time to visit his camp. The group circled with their head men for an impromptu council, which included some of the elders and chiefs, as well as a few of those who had been stealing horses.

"These white men want their horses," Bear Hunter said.

"They already had those horses. Now we have them," one of the young men laughed.

"How much trouble for The People do you think those horses are worth?" Bear Hunter asked.

"What do you mean? The Mormons will not do anything. They never do anything."

"You are wrong, you young fool," Sagwitch said. "The Mormons do many things. Most of the food that goes into that smart mouth of yours came from the Mormons."

"So what?" another of the young men said. "They have plenty. Besides, they only give us enough to stave off the hunger. Never enough to fill our bellies."

Sagwitch said, "How much longer do you think they will keep staving off your hunger if you keep stealing their horses?"

The young men had no answer for that. Bear Hunter waited, letting the silence grow uncomfortable.

"Here is what I think," he finally said. "We will send six of our people with this Mormon army to help them find their horses. It would be well if some were recovered. You know where this last bunch was taken. It has been many hours, and white men will understand that the trail has gone cold. But I think if you try, you can find enough horses to make them happy."

With that, Bear Hunter turned on his heel and walked back to where the Mormons waited, the Minute Men too impatient even to dismount. He explained that, even though none of the men in this camp knew anything about the horses, they were sending out some skilled and experienced trackers to help find them.

"The Shoshoni stole between thirty and forty horses and got about a twelve-hour head start on the Minute Men," Mormon leader Peter Maughan told Brigham Young in a letter reporting the expedition. "They could only recover nine or ten of the animals. Six friendly Indians (if I may be allowed the expression) went along with our men. I suppose they have stolen one hundred horses in three weeks. What makes it worse is that those who pretend to be friendly will harbor those scamps about their wickiups until they get their plans laid for stealing. At the same time, we have been giving them tons of flour and beef. It does seem to me that the Indians are determined to drive us to hostile measures."

CHAPTER TWELVE

In the cold nights and days of the camp where Sagwitch and his followers spent most winters, the edges of *Boa Ogoi* froze solid. Every morning, the boys tending the horses chopped drinking holes for the animals through thick, white ice. Farther out in the stream, the ice thinned translucent and turned to lace, then filigree, as it neared the main strength of the current, where slush and chunks of ice shed upstream swept along in the flow.

As rivers go, *Boa Ogoi* did not amount to much. In the well-watered East, it would not even merit the name "river." A run, more likely. A creek. Or—most appropriate given its destiny—a kill. But out West, the stream the white men named the Bear is a mighty river and distinctive in its ways.

It is the largest watercourse in North America that never reaches an ocean.

It ends less than one hundred miles from where it rises, but flows some five hundred miles in the trip, draining seven and a half thousand square miles of mountains and valleys as it goes.

According to maps, the horseshoe shape of the Bear River starts in Utah, crosses the border into Wyoming, sneaks into Utah again but soon returns to Wyoming, leaves there finally for Idaho, then turns back into Utah, never to leave again.

By the time the stream entered the consciousness of white trappers and mountain men early in the second decade of the nineteenth century, the Bear River, the *Boa Ogoi,* and its basins and canyons and mountains and valleys had been among the

73

homelands of the *Newe*—The People—the Shoshoni—for eight centuries, at least.

Some forty or fifty miles as the crow flies upstream from where the Bear River empties into the Great Salt Lake, a small, occasional stream called Beaver Creek meanders onto the river plain and joins the river. A short way to the south, hot springs seep out of the ground and, on the coldest days, spew plumes of steam into the frigid air. The warm water baths and high sheltering bluffs that protect the mile-wide plain from the worst of wind and storm made this place a popular and often used winter camp for Sagwitch's people and other bands of the Shoshoni.

Too many used the place that winter.

CHAPTER THIRTEEN

January 1863

This place where Beaver Creek joins *Boa Ogoi* lies but a few miles north of the forty-second parallel. Squatting beside the streaming water of the big river and lost in thought, Bear Hunter was unaware of that fact of latitude. Had he known, he would not have cared. The place had been part of his people's homeland time out of mind, and boundary lines upon the land imagined by white men mattered not to him.

But such lines, and that one in particular, would have made all the difference to the Mormons thereabouts and perhaps the soldiers, had they known its location. For that line placed the Shoshoni camp outside the political influence of Utah Territory.

That imaginary line of latitude, in fact, placed the camp firmly in what would be Idaho Territory, soon to be carved out of the Territory of Washington, itself created from Oregon Territory, ownership of which had lately been the subject of some controversy between Great Britain and the United States of America, and before that a bone of contention picked over by the Americans, the French, the British, and the Russians. So the camp was now, in the American way of thinking, the responsibility of political appointees headquartered far away in Olympia who neither knew nor cared about the place or its people.

But the Mormons who had settled on that ancestral Shoshoni land thought they were still and all in Utah, and the government in Salt Lake City thought so, too, and so did the United

States Army garrisoned at Camp Douglas in that city, and so they all behaved as if the place was a Utah place.

And Bear Hunter did not care. Nor did the water in which his mind was lost care, flowing unknowingly as it did from one sphere of political influence to another.

The People had just come to this place to settle in for the winter, as they did most winters and had done since before Bear Hunter could remember. It was a quiet place, with surrounding bluffs sheltering the camp from the worst of the cold winds and snowstorms that blew regularly across the land.

Most of the lodges were pitched in the place where the ravine that confined Beaver Creek emerged from between the high bluffs, then followed the ravine and the creek a short way out onto the open ground of the river bottoms. A mile wide at this place, the flood plain spread north and south and widened as the *Boa Ogoi* wandered back and forth.

The horse herd was well fed, pawing through snow as necessary to reach the cured meadow grass below. The hot springs south of the village made bathing a pleasant task. The village of Franklin was near enough for convenience in obtaining supplies but far enough away to allow the Mormons and The People to live in their separate worlds, unmolested.

That, at least, was the theory by which the world turned. But Bear Hunter knew that theory and reality were drawing further and further apart. Some of the Shoshoni had indiscriminately killed white men and stolen goods and rustled livestock. Some of the whites had abused the Shoshoni, killing them and driving them from their homeland.

And then there were the soldiers.

The entry of the California Volunteers into the Great Basin last summer brought with it a ruthlessness, a cruelty in killing the like of which he had never seen. There had been the killings on the Humboldt. Bear Hunter, himself, knew he had narrowly escaped death when taken by McGarry and his troops when they were hunting that white boy. And there had been the killing of the captives at the place on the river the white men called Empey's Ferry.

All this had happened in just a few rounds of the moon, and Bear Hunter did not think these soldiers were finished. But, he hoped, the winter here on the *Boa Ogoi* would be a peaceful one, the coming Warm Dance joyful, the weather temperate, The People content, the young men pacific.

But, Bear Hunter feared there was something else in the whine of the wind in the winter sky over the bluffs above the *Boa Ogoi*.

The screams of the children carried sharp and clear through the cold air. Bear Hunter left the warmth of his lodge to watch as a young girl on a stiff, dried deer hide slid and spun uncontrolled down the steep hill above the village. Another child, whether boy or girl he could not tell, pushed off on the same course from the hilltop as others climbed up for their turns, dragging hides behind. Out on the bottoms, older boys, on horseback, dragged hides tied to the ends of ropes at high speed across the flats, whip-snaking friends across the snowy ground. Other children knocked stuffed rawhide balls about with sticks, playing a game whose rules or purpose he could not discern.

Nearly a thousand—maybe more—of the *Newe*—The People—were gathered at the winter camp on the *Boa Ogoi* for the annual Warm Dance. A festive time, the Warm Dance was a period of celebration, of storytelling, of camaraderie, of competition, of councils, of music, and of dancing to hasten the end of winter and invite clement weather to the land of the Shoshoni. And to offer up kindly and grateful thoughts to the Great Spirit.

Most adults, like Bear Hunter, enjoyed the relative relaxation and leisure of the winter camp and the Warm Dance. He could only admire the energy and enthusiasm of the children, the recollection of his own such exuberance dimmed by the passage of years. Nowadays, his idea of a good time tended more toward a drink of hot mint tea on a soft buffalo robe next to a glowing fire in the warm tipi of his family, or in the inviting lodge of a friend.

Bear Hunter's band had traditionally wintered in this place for time out of mind. Rare was the winter they chose another. Sagwitch and his people were regulars, as were those who followed Lehi. Sanpitch with his band and Pocatello's sizable following sometimes wintered here and, as they were doing now, almost always spent an extended visit to celebrate the Warm Dance. Others of the *Newe* came for the Warm Dance from the deserts to the west, still others—Washakie's people—from the east, and more from the mountains far to the north.

Not all was fun and games at this Warm Dance, however. Some of the councils among the chiefs had been contentious. Pocatello, especially, had been criticized for not doing more to keep his young men under control.

"The People have been killing the whites for many years," Pocatello pointed out to the assembled chiefs. "My band. Your bands. Those of our cousins to the east and the west, and those up north on the Salmon River. Nothing is new."

Sagwitch said, "Something is new. The soldiers are back."

"We have had soldiers before."

"That is true, Pocatello. But these soldiers are different. They are eager to kill. And they have already attacked us more since coming into the country from the west last summer than the soldiers from the east did in all the years they were here."

Sagwitch's observations were true. From 1858 until it disbanded in 1861, the army under the command of Albert Sidney Johnston at Camp Floyd in Utah Territory comprised the largest concentration of troops in the whole of the United

States of America at the time. Since the war with the Mormons never materialized, Johnston turned his attention to Indian fighting. But, while his troops had engaged Shoshoni bands in battle on several occasions, the army seemed to flit hither and yon fighting Utes, Paiutes, Gosiutes, and Shoshoni with no concerted efforts or noticeable plans or strategies. In some sense, Johnston seemed to consider retaliation for Indian depredations the responsibility of the Mormons.

Throughout the stay of Johnston's army, Shoshoni attacks on emigrant trains, mail stations, and express routes grew more frequent and intense. At the same time, relations with Mormon settlers in Cache Valley and elsewhere on Shoshoni homelands deteriorated, and bloodshed increased. And the chiefs in council at the Warm Dance and the warriors who followed them had been right in the thick of it.

Bear Hunter, the oldest and most respected of the chiefs in the eastern valleys of the Great Basin, and recognized as war chief over them all, agreed with Sagwitch. "The soldiers here before now could not make up their minds what to do. These from California know what they want—they want to kill us. And now, unlike the last time, the Mormons may be on their side."

"The Mormons will not hurt us," Pocatello said. "They think we are their brothers and want us to join them in their church. What do they care about the soldiers? They do not even like them."

"It is true the Mormons do not like the American soldiers. But your young men have stolen so many of their animals and killed so many travelers that now they are afraid of us and do not want to give us food."

Pocatello scoffed. "If they will not give us food, we will take it. They have ruined our land. Their cattle graze where we once gathered seeds and roots. They have killed and scared away all the game so we can't even hunt. My people do not intend to starve, so we will take the food we need from those who keep us from getting our own."

"You make it hard to argue, Pocatello," Bear Hunter said.

Sagwitch said, "But that does not change anything. We must be friends with the Mormons and avoid trouble. If we do not, they will be friends with the soldiers. They do not like the cruelty of this man McGarry and his leader Connor. They are not happy with the way the soldiers have slaughtered captives and the unarmed. But they do not like the way The People have killed travelers on the road and stolen cattle and horses and frightened their women. When it comes down to it, the Mormons will ally themselves with the American soldiers and not The People."

"So what? What do we care?"

"Are you blind with rage, Pocatello?" said Bear Hunter. "Brigham Young has done much to protect us from the Americans. He has given us guns against the wishes of the soldiers. He tells his people to get along with us and share their food. If the Mormons turn against us, we are doomed. Maybe they have already turned their faces from us. We cannot withstand the soldiers and the Mormons, too."

Pocatello's face hardened. "My people must eat. And we will take food where we find it. Maybe if we kill enough of the Americans on the roads and steal enough from the Mormons, they will all go away."

Sagwitch smiled, but there was no mirth in the expression. He shook his head slowly and said, "They will not go away. And we cannot stop more from coming. All your young men are accomplishing with all their killing is to make the Americans mad. And now the Mormons are mad, too."

The summer of 1862 had been a busy one for the Shoshoni inclined to harass and kill the whites. Some of these killers were among the bands on the *Boa Ogoi*, some with other bands of The People—the Eastern Shoshoni, the Fort Hall, the Lemhi, the Western Shoshoni, the Boise, the Bruneau. No matter the band, many among the Shoshoni had been active and aggressive.

The Smith-Kinkaid emigrant party had been all but wiped out on the trail between the Bear River and Raft River—wiped out save a man named Smith, who somehow made his way south to a Mormon settlement with an arrow in his back.

At a place near Soda Springs, where the Bear River abandons its northern journey and turns south toward its eventual demise in the brine of the Great Salt Lake, three wagon trains were plundered by Shoshoni warriors from bands led by Pocatello and Lehi, and many of the emigrants were killed.

Ten whites were killed in fighting along the Snake River at a place that would thereafter be known as Massacre Rocks.

Three dead men and their abandoned wagons were found at the parting of the California and Oregon Trails on the Snake River Plain.

The bodies of five miners on the road to the Salmon River country were left beside the trail, scalped and mutilated.

Fifteen well-armed traders were attacked near Raft River: six were killed; nine barely escaped with their lives through a chance meeting with an emigrant train.

By September, the Shoshoni raiders had effectively closed the trails, and James Doty, federal appointee over Indian affairs in Utah Territory, actively discouraged travel. Throughout the summer and continuing through the fall and winter, he had hounded Congress and his bureaucratic superiors for money and more money and still more money for gifts and annuities and food to placate the Indians.

Instead, he got Colonel Patrick Edward Connor and the California Volunteers.

"Sagwitch, sometimes I think you care more about the Mormons than you do The People," Pocatello said.

"That is nonsense," Bear Hunter said in the younger chief's defense. "He wants our people to live, just as you do. But he sees a different future than you do. Sagwitch, what do you think will happen?"

"I think if we keep killing the whites, the soldiers will punish us. But I do not think they will kill us all. Like they have done before, they will want the killers, and if we give them up they will leave us alone."

"That has worked sometimes before," Bear Hunter said. "But I do not think it will work with these soldiers. They took me prisoner under a white flag and threatened to kill me when I had done nothing wrong. They killed those Shoshoni men when they were tied up and sent their bodies down the river. Those men had done nothing. And you have heard of other innocent People they have killed. These soldiers are happy to kill the first person they find for revenge, rather than seeking out the guilty party."

"Maybe," said Sagwitch.

"Do you think they will be happy taking a few prisoners now and then if our people keep killing whites?"

"Maybe."

"I wish I thought so, Sagwitch, but I think if Pocatello and the rest of us cannot control our warriors, and they keep killing whites, the soldiers will not leave us alone until they have driven us out of the country or killed us all."

Bear Hunter knew Sagwitch hoped for peace but did not think either Pocatello or Lehi would do anything to discourage the slaughter. Their blood was as hot these days as that of the young warriors in seeking revenge or asserting their rights. Even now, since the last full moon, while they should have been tucked away in their lodges staying warm, some of their

Shoshoni warriors had been out killing whites.

Two freighters on the Cache Valley road had been murdered just weeks ago. Eight miners had been killed further north. And, only days ago, a marauding band of Pocatello's warriors visiting the Warm Dance had encountered a party of southbound miners just a few miles south of Bear Hunter's village. He asked the chief to explain.

"Those stupid white men were lost," Pocatello laughed. "They were taking their three wagons along that new road that goes past here just a mile to the west. You know the one. They should have crossed the *Boa Ogoi* at that ford just a little way downstream of here but were so dumb they missed it. So they ended up on the wrong side of the river, stumbling around out in the boggy ground across the river from that Mormon town, Richmond.

"There were eight of them. Three took horses and crossed over to the town to get help. Some of our warriors came across the ones who were left and gave them a good scare. They only wanted to have some fun, I think, and watch those white men squirm a little. They pushed them around, threatened to cut off their private parts with skinning knives, that sort of thing. You know how young men will behave. One of the white men shat himself, they say," Pocatello said with a laugh.

"After a while, they got tired of playing. Some of the young men took what they wanted from the wagons and stole the horses, while some of the warriors hung around to see what would happen next. Then, the other white men came back with some help from the town and sniveled and begged to have their animals back. Having had their fun, those young men went and brought back some of the horses.

"So the white men got the wagons over to the east side of the river, and our warriors decided to have some more fun and started taking target practice. One of them got lucky and shot one of the white men dead. You should have seen the rest of them run for town! Those white men won't be bothering The People anymore. And I think it will be a good, long time before they come anywhere near the *Boa Ogoi* country again."

"That is the same way I heard the story from others, Pocatello," Bear Hunter said. "I guess there is nothing wrong with the young men having a little fun now and then, but the white men—even the Mormons—are not laughing about that one. As a matter of fact, they are mad as hell. Sanpitch is just back from talking to Brigham Young in Salt Lake City. He had already heard about what your young men did. Say what the leader of the Mormons told you, Sanpitch."

Sanpitch said, "First, I will say that my people are worried. They do not want to fight with the Mormons unless they have to. So I asked Brigham Young how to make things peaceful among our people again. But he did not want to talk about it. He said the Mormons in Cache Valley have had enough trouble from us, and, if the American solders come to fight, the Mormons might just pitch in and help them. I did not like to hear this."

Neither did the other chiefs. But they would hear things even more troubling before long. They would hear the dream of the old man Tin Dup.

CHAPTER FOURTEEN

"You're sure, Brother Brigham, of what you're asking of me?"

"Yes. It is my will. And, I believe, the will of the Lord in this matter."

Porter Rockwell inhaled long and slow and let the air escape the same way. The chair on which he sat in the office of Brigham Young in the Beehive House scraped the floor as Rockwell stood. He worried his hat in his hands for a moment then paced a quick circuit of the room, stopped before the president of all the Mormons and God's prophet upon the earth, opened his mouth as if to speak, but instead bit if off and circled the room again.

The clerk, sitting quietly at the rolltop desk against the wall, watched Rockwell in wonder. Most folks—Mormon and gentile alike—stood in respectful silence before this emperor of the Great Basin, sat only when invited, spoke only when spoken to, left when dismissed, and, most certainly, did not question President Young. Brother Brigham liked it like that.

"What is it, Port? What troubles you? Come on, spit it out, man."

"I've knowed you a long time, Brother Brigham."

"I know it, Port. Go on."

"I've did your bidding for better or worse since you took over the reins of this here church."

Brigham Young waited for whatever was next, his usual stern countenance betraying nothing.

"Well, I just don't see it," Rockwell said when the silence grew too uncomfortable—which was not long, since the man tended to be uncomfortable in any place where pomp and ceremony were the usual order of things. "Hell, Brig!" he said, prompting a gasp from the clerk, who rarely witnessed such familiarity. "It weren't but a few years ago you sent me out to lead men *against* the armies of the U. S. of A. and now you want to send me out *with* the damn soldier boys?"

"I suppose that sums it up, Port."

"But why?"

"As usual, because you are the best man for the job. You are one to be relied on. Colonel Connor has been asking around—although he would not deign to ask me directly—for the best scout in the territory to guide this expedition. You need not be reminded that that would be you."

"And you know nothing more of Connor's plans?"

"Only what I've told you. His intention is to subdue the Shoshoni who have been troubling emigrants and miners and other travelers. He is also concerned for our people settled there, but less so. He will be accompanied by Marshal Gibbs, who has murder warrants to serve on Bear Hunter and Sagwitch and some others. Port, do you know Peter Maughan?"

"I do. Knew him over Tooele way some years back. Don't know what become of him."

"He was sent to settle the Cache Valley and has made a good job of it—a whole string of communities is there now, and the Saints are prospering as well as can be expected in a place of such long winters. From my correspondence with Brother Maughan, I am informed that the Shoshoni have been acting saucy in their relations with the Saints. There have been several incidents. I'll not burden you with details. Suffice it to say I believe the time has come to send a message. Our intentions concerning the Shoshoni, as with all our Lamanite brothers, are peaceful. But our people will not tolerate being abused."

This time, it was Brigham Young who grew uncomfortable with the silence.

"Port, I would consider it a favor if you would report to Colonel Connor at his headquarters up at the camp and do his bidding."

Rockwell let himself out as the clerk's pen nib scratched furiously in the recording of the business.

Camp Douglas sprawled across a gently sloping beach that had not known water for millions of years. Wave motion of Lake Bonneville, which once covered this part of the Great Basin a thousand feet deep before receding down the ages, had laid sediments against the wall of the Wasatch Mountains, stepping down to the valley floor in a broad staircase. From heights thus created, Camp Douglas looked over the city below, the center of which lay three miles west.

By the time Rockwell rode across the slushy parade ground to the headquarters building, Colonel Patrick Edward Connor had long been watching his coming. Still, he made no move to welcome or even greet the man he considered a coarse hooligan, an outlaw, a killer, and a treasonous traitor. Then again, that last was true of Mormons one and all, to his way of thinking. Nevertheless, Porter Rockwell was said to be the best scout within five hundred miles, and perhaps farther.

Connor instructed his aide to allow the ruffian to cool his heels in the outer office, then summon Captain Hoyt and Major McGarry and, once the officers arrived, show all three men into his office.

The colonel continued to busy himself gazing out the window until a knock at his door announced the entry of the three men. As always, Captain Sam Hoyt was all spit and polish. Major Edward McGarry, while properly uniformed, was his usual casual self, marching just at the edge of sloppiness.

The civilian Rockwell was well across that line. From run-over boots to the homespun shirt and stained coat, to the wide-brimmed hat he did not bother to remove, which covered long hair tied with a twine at the nape of his neck, to the shaggy beard hanging to his chest, he appeared the very picture of slovenliness to the prim and proper Connor.

Connor had been given to understand that the untrimmed hair and beard resulted from a Samson-like promise from God through Joseph Smith that Rockwell would be protected from harm if unshorn. The colonel did not think he would allow himself such an unkempt appearance even if instructed by heaven. Be that as it may, the man would be on the payroll for his skills as an outdoorsman, not his sartorial accomplishments.

The two officers snapped to attention and saluted, Hoyt with more enthusiasm than McGarry. Rockwell leaned himself against the wall near the fireplace in this, the first and only building worthy of the name at the camp. It served Connor as both headquarters and quarters. The men under his command were as yet billeted in wall tents on log foundations and cave-like dugouts.

"Major McGarry. Captain Hoyt. At ease, gentlemen," Connor said. "We'll not stand on ceremony. And you there, I assume, would be the infamous Orrin Porter Rockwell."

McGarry winced when he heard the name and cast a hard glance at Rockwell, who nodded once in the colonel's direction but did not bother to reply otherwise.

"I have heard much about you over the years, Rockwell. I believe you spent some time in my adopted state of California, back in the gold rush years," Connor said.

Again, Rockwell's reply consisted of a single nod.

"Are you loyal to the Union?"

The surprising question did not occasion a nod, merely a

perplexed look.

"The war, Mister Rockwell. What are your thoughts on the war?"

Port ruminated on the query for a moment before saying, "Can't say I think about it much at all."

"Surely it is your wish that the Union prevail."

"Well, I guess I wish the same as most folks hereabouts."

"That being?"

"Seems to us them northern states and southern states are hell bent on destroying each other. We wish them both luck."

Connor reddened at the reply, reinforcing as it did the notion he had carried since before his arrival here: that if the Mormons were not disloyal to the Union cause in any outright way, they were far from what one might consider loyal. All their pious jabber about the divinity of the Constitution didn't fool him one bit. He believed they would bolt the Union at first opportunity should it appear to be to their advantage, and he was determined to see that the opportunity never presented itself. But just now, today, there were more pressing matters.

"Mister Rockwell," Connor continued through clenched teeth, "despite your ambivalence about the sanctity of the Union and your questionable loyalty to your government, I will demand your unquestioning loyalty to my command for the duration of your employ by this army. Am I clear?"

In reply, Rockwell offered the now familiar single nod.

"Let me explain our purpose in seeking your services. On the morrow, the twenty-second of January, Captain Hoyt here will leave for the Cache Valley. Accompanying him will be seventy-two troops of infantry and a twelve-man detachment of cavalry. These men will escort fifteen supply wagons and two mountain howitzers, concealed, of course, in the wagons.

"Word will be broadcast throughout the territory that their purpose will be the safe conduct of a wagon train load of grain out of Cache Valley, protecting said train from the predatory Indians who frequent the area, killing and plundering travelers. No other explanation is to be offered. Am I clear?"

Again, Rockwell nodded.

Connor then explained how, under cover of darkness three days later, the colonel himself and Major McGarry would leave the camp at the head of two hundred and twenty cavalrymen and dragoons with the intention of joining forces with the previously dispatched infantry on the night of January twenty-eighth near Franklin, the northernmost settlement in Cache Valley. Connor made it clear that the cavalry would travel in secret so far as possible, and that no notice of nor explanation for their march would be offered.

"I intend to surprise the Shoshoni in their camp and punish them severely. Your role in this affair will be to accompany Major McGarry and myself on the cavalry march, serving as guide and acquiring such services as may be required along the way from your churchmen. Upon our rendezvous with Captain Hoyt at Franklin, you will locate and reconnoiter the Indian camp and report. Your counsel on tactics may be requested. Maybe not. If not asked, you will not offer. You will accompany our return to this camp, again obtaining such assistance along the way as proves necessary. You will be paid for your services at the rate of five dollars per day. Am I clear?"

Rockwell nodded.

"Have you any questions?"

"What about Gibbs?"

"Gibbs?"

"Ike Gibbs. The territorial marshal. I was told he would be along to serve warrants on some of the Shoshoni chiefs. He's to arrest them on account of the killing of that miner up by Richmond. The ones he was travelin' with swore out complaints with the judge, and he gave Gibbs the warrants."

"Ah, yes, the marshal," Connor said. "I have told him he is welcome to accompany us and so are his warrants. I have also told him his warrants will not be necessary, as I do not intend to take any prisoners."

Three pairs of eyes bored into Rockwell as Connor, McGarry, and Hoyt allowed this last to sink in. Connor broke the silence.

"If there is nothing else, Mister Rockwell, my aide will assist you in signing the proper payroll forms."

Rockwell nodded. He shouldered himself upright from his leaning place against the wall and saw himself out of Connor's office. Expecting him, the aide in the outer office tapped excess ink off a pen nib against the edge of the inkwell, indicated the place where the paper should be signed, and handed him the pen.

Rockwell scratched out a bold black *X*.

CHAPTER FIFTEEN

McGarry stared out the window as Colonel Connor's instructions to Captain Hoyt deteriorated into a murmur. For all the attention he paid, the conversation might as well have taken place on the moon as in the same room.

As he watched, Porter Rockwell left the building, loosened his mount's tie rope from the hitch rail, then mounted up and kicked the horse into a canter across the parade ground. The sonofabitch can't wait to get back to Brigham Young and tell him what we're up to, McGarry thought. It was common knowledge in Utah Territory that there were no secrets from the Mormons, and what any Mormon knew was soon shared with "Brother Brigham," as these misguided lunatics called their leader.

Given his way, McGarry would save the Indians for later. He would, instead, march every cavalry trooper and every infantryman straight down the hill to Mormon headquarters and arrest Young and every other Mormon in a position of authority. And he would not hesitate to shoot any of them, or any of their followers, who objected.

Despite every effort to establish federal control and an influential territorial government, the true and only power lay in the hands of church leaders. To McGarry's way of thinking, it was a damn shame Colonel Albert Sydney Johnston had not done the job he was sent here to do in 1857. The Utah War, they called it. Sorry damn excuse for a war.

Connor shared his opinion of these so-called Saints, McGarry knew, but political considerations and imprecise orders constrained the commander from doing what needed to be done. Hell, thought McGarry, with Washington up to its ass in secessionist problems, the California Volunteers could exterminate the damn Mormons, and no one would even care.

And now, McGarry was expected to follow Porter Rockwell's tracks on a march to Cache Valley. Then again, he thought, riding behind Brigham's "Destroying Angel" might provide an opportunity to back shoot the murderous cutthroat.

"Major McGarry."

Through the gentle alcoholic haze in which he perpetually dwelled, McGarry thought he heard someone calling his name.

"Major! Dammit, McGarry, would you kindly give us the pleasure of your company?"

He turned from the window and realized it was the colonel calling. The fact that Connor's face had taken on the same fiery shade as his hair and side whiskers was evidence that it had not been the commander's first summons.

"Sorry, sir," McGarry said. "I was watching Rockwell ride away and got lost estimating distance and wind direction and muzzle velocity."

Connor erupted in laughter, his anger washed away in the flood of the major's peculiar comment.

"I take it you are not a fan of the principal henchman of all the Mormons."

"No, Colonel, I can't say as I am. As a matter of fact, the only circumstance under which I would like to see him again is if he was twisting at the end of a rope. Or maybe layin' on the ground bleeding out from a bullet wound from my sidearm."

"All in good time, Major. All in good time. As for now, I believe Rockwell may prove useful to our cause. I have made numerous inquiries throughout the territory, and he is, almost without exception, considered to be the best guide and scout available, as well as being a particularly resourceful man in tight situations."

"Still and all, I do not like the very idea of the man and would rather not have to abide his presence on this expedition. After all, it's not as if I can't find the way north in the dark, or that I don't know where to look for Cache Valley."

"I take your point. But Rockwell will accompany us, nonetheless. His knowledge of the area surpasses yours and will reduce the time necessary to locate the savages in their warrens," Connor said. "We shall utilize his expertise and assistance wherever and whenever it proves practical. Am I clear?"

"Yes, Colonel."

"Now, back to business. Captain Hoyt, please bring the major up to date, if you will. It seems he has been otherwise occupied."

Sam Hoyt had been watching the exchange between Connor and McGarry with a bemused expression. He did not know either officer well but was impressed with Connor's businesslike manner and no-nonsense attitude.

McGarry, on the other hand, was an enigma. The man drank a good deal, Hoyt knew. Too much. And yet he seemed able to function normally and carry out his duties unimpaired. When he thought about it, Hoyt did not know if he had never seen the man drunk, or never seen him sober. From what he had heard from the men and from junior officers, McGarry was cruel and heartless with the enemy, and downright mean in dealing with his own troops. And yet the colonel relied on McGarry more than any other officer in the command, and he was always first choice for carrying out operations against the Indians.

Hoyt abandoned his straying thoughts and snapped back to his usual seriousness and efficiency at Connor's command.

"Yes, sir. You will recall, Major McGarry, that I will depart here in the morning with a company of infantry, fifteen baggage wagons, and the two howitzers. Our march will be a deliberate one; we intend to make only fifteen to twenty miles a day. If, as some suspect, there is a big storm brewing, even that distance might tax our abilities.

"This evening, the wagons will be loaded with camp and field gear, twenty days' rations, ammunition for a full complement of carbines and sidearms, and one hundred shells for the howitzers, etcetera, and so on. I'll not bore you with further details on the nature of our supplies and ammunition.

"As the colonel has said, we will rendezvous with your cavalry at some point in the northern Cache Valley, as near as is practicable to the town of Franklin, without revealing your presence. Our march, of course, will be out in the open and our presence made known to the Shoshoni. Our intention, it will be let slip to the Indians, will be to offer protection for a grain shipment out of the valley. That, of course is pretense, our presence a diversion to disguise the coming of your cavalry troops."

"Thank you, Captain," Connor said. "Your cavalry companies, Major, will depart after dark three days later. I will accompany you. Each trooper is to draw three days' rations of cooked food to be carried in haversacks. We will bivouac as necessary along the way, eliminating the need for camp equipment. That should not require serious hardship for the men until we join forces with Captain Hoyt and his baggage wagons.

"Additionally, each man will be issued one canteen of medicinal whiskey for the trail. As you are well aware, Major, I do not approve of alcohol, especially while on duty, but in this instance it should serve to comfort the men. Our journey would likely be long and difficult in the best of circumstances. Since we will attempt it—nay accomplish it—at night and in winter, a wee dram of drink will not be amiss.

"As to armament, each trooper will be issued forty rounds of carbine ammunition and thirty rounds each of pistol ammunition for use in the field."

McGarry digested what Connor said for a moment then observed, "That's seventy rounds per man, Colonel, for four companies of cavalry! I am not much for ciphering, but that must be more than ten thousand rounds."

"Closer to sixteen thousand, Major."

"That's a hell of a lot to carry, sir. You must be figuring there's a bunch of Shoshoni up there who need killing."

"Indeed, Major. But let us not forget that the men who will be firing that ammunition recently expended more than fifty rounds merely to dispatch at close range four bound prisoners."

McGarry winced at the reference to the execution of Shoshoni captives he had ordered at Empey's Ferry less than two months earlier.

"Word is, that particular style of shooting did not sit well with the Shoshoni and has gotten their blood up. So, I doubt they will be so accommodating as to stand bound this time," Connor said. "In all probability, it will not be as easy for your troopers to get clear a shot. And there is every possibility the Indians will shoot back. Am I clear?"

"Yes, sir," McGarry said. "Point taken."

CHAPTER SIXTEEN

Had one been abroad on the land the night of the twenty-fifth of January 1863 (an odd supposition given the inhospitable state of the weather), the rip and tear of the wind from the north would have filled one's ears to the exclusion of all other sound. Still, at a certain point, the awareness of a great sound would have been there—a sound sometimes felt and sometimes, almost, heard.

Imagine: the drumbeat of more than a thousand hooves on a long trot over the frozen road rolling in waves through the shallow depths of the earth.

Consider: from time to time an almost imperceptible lull in the wind's pressure, and, in that slight dampening of the roar, space is made for the dim but persistent rattle of hundreds of bridle bit chains; for the grunts of hard-breathing horses gulping for supplementary breath; of chilled saddle leather squeaking and shivering with every shift in stirrup weight.

Had one been on the road that night, such mystifying and unlikely suggestions of sound would grow and grow until one could no longer resist turning to search the dark road behind for the source of this spectral noise.

Then, one must make haste to the side of the road and watch in silent wonder as Companies A, H, K, and M of the Second Cavalry of the California Volunteers of the United States Army appear out of the blowing snow to thunder past in a seemingly endless torrent, only to disappear again into the storm ahead.

And the sound of the mysterious parade trails away on the night wind in a diminishing wake.

With tucked chin, hunched shoulders, and squinted eyes, Porter Rockwell rode into the teeth of the storm. Readying for the expedition, he had strapped tapaderos over the stirrup fronts on his California stock saddle to protect against wind and snow and wet, as well as provide warmth. Three pairs of heavy socks made his high-topped boots uncomfortably snug. He wore long johns under two pairs of trousers under wooly chaps. He barely felt the reins through heavy, fur-lined mittens. Two wool shirts, a blanket-lined canvas coat, and a long heavy coat fashioned from buffalo robes rounded out his attire, save a long woolen muffler wrapped over the top of his head and around his neck and face, serving the dual purpose of warmth and keeping his wide-brimmed felt hat from kiting away in the stiff wind. To add even more warmth, Rockwell had lashed a fat bedroll across the forks of the saddle and another roll behind the cantle.

And still the cold cut through him like a saber. He pitied the cavalry troopers on flat saddles with open stirrups and skimpy blankets.

They had ridden out of Camp Douglas more than two hundred and twenty men strong at nightfall and struck the road north. Colonel Connor's plan was to maintain secrecy and surprise by traveling only at night, meeting up with the previously dispatched infantry troops three nights hence at the northern end of Cache Valley.

The road was a well traveled one, the main route linking the Mormon settlements along the fringe of the Wasatch mountain range, so Rockwell's services as guide were not required at this juncture. Burrowing his head deeper into his shoulders and the collar of the buffalo-robe coat, Rockwell allowed his mind to

wander back over an earlier encounter with the United States
Army.

It had been just past five years ago, late September of 1857,
that Rockwell had led Mormon raiders in the first action of the
Utah War. Due to a series of mishaps, misunderstandings,
miscommunication, and all-around ill feelings and bad behavior
on the parts of both federal officials sent to govern the territory
and the Mormon leaders there, President James Buchanan had
declared the polygamous and politically independent Mormons
in open rebellion against the nation. Some three thousand
troops had been dispatched to the territory to compel obedi-
ence under force of arms.

Brigham Young, whose term as territorial governor had long
since expired but who continued to act in the office until a
replacement arrived, was not informed of the expedition
through official channels. Although well aware of the gathering
army and its mission through rumor and informal communication, the first reliable news of the approaching army was carried
to him by Rockwell, returning from a mail run to the east.

The Mormon leader considered the advancing soldiers nothing more than an illegal invasion at best and a lawless mob at
worst and declared martial law. Standing before the assembled
Saints he declared "Woe, woe, woe to that man who comes here
unlawfully to interfere with my affairs. Woe, woe to those men
who come here to unlawfully meddle with me and this people."

Young's fiery assistant, Heber Kimball, was even more color-
ful. "God Almighty helping me, I will fight until there is not a
drop of blood in my veins," he said. "Good God! I have *wives*
enough to whip the United States!"

The Mormon militia, still called the Nauvoo Legion from its
days in that Illinois city, was activated and preparations for war
undertaken. As federal troops drew nearer and winter approached, Young determined the best strategy for the time being

was to keep the army out of the populated places of Utah and force them to winter cold, alone, and hungry on the high plains.

A number of ranging bands were organized to carry out guerilla raids, one of which was placed under Rockwell's command. Young's instructions were to burn feed and forage, destroy supply trains, and carry out any other action—short of killing, unless in self-defense—to harass and delay the government troops.

At a place called Pacific Springs, in what is now Wyoming, Rockwell and his small band crept up on bivouacked troops in the wee hours of the morning. The primary weapon in the raid was a large brass cowbell, whose loud clapper, accompanied by war whoops and gun shots, rudely awakened the soldiers as the mounted Mormons rushed the camp. The soldiers stumbled out of their sleep to find their pack mules hightailing it across the prairie, driven on by the raiders who had accomplished their purpose.

But the Mormon victory was short-lived. Not yet a mile away, Rockwell watched flabbergasted as his conquest crumbled. For starters, the bell mare's lead rope tangled in the brush, and when she halted much of the herd did, too. Then, an alert bugler among the troopers sounded "Stable Call," and the rest of the mules immediately reversed direction. Neither the tongue lashing nor the lash of whips they received from the Mormons could turn the stubborn mules away from the meal they expected to be awaiting them back at camp.

Not exactly the shot heard round the world, that opening salvo of the Utah War. Rockwell smiled at the memory. But it hadn't seemed funny at the time. Now, here he was cold to the bone and on a night march with troops of the same abusive government that once was his enemy.

And that didn't seem funny either.

CHAPTER SEVENTEEN

Confusion, if not chaos, came to Connor's cavalry with the break of day. The slowly growing light knew no source. There was no ribbon of dawn, no sunrise, only a flat, dull gray slowly displacing darkness. The breathing of men and mounts alike was labored in the chilled air, the exhalation building a hazy, humid cloud.

Men, some dismounted and others still horseback, milled aimlessly in the storm. It had been snowing when they left Camp Douglas, and it had not stopped through the long winter night, the accumulation growing ever deeper as the troops rode north into the storm. And the wind—pummeling and pelting the men full in the face for most of the night.

Many men's feet, locked into stirrups, lacked all feeling, entombed in windblown snow frozen into blocks of ice. Frosted mustaches and beards, entwined inches deep under snow and ice and drool and the crystallized humidity of exhalation, locked mouths closed. Fingers, inflexible, clung helplessly and without purpose to stiffened leather reins.

Had anyone cared to read a thermometer, the measure of the storm would have to be taken by numbers well below the mark indicating zero degrees.

Tucked as they were into the maw of Box Elder Canyon, the cavalry found some relief from the wind. But still the snow fell. Officers rode through the troops ordering, directing misplaced men to where their units were assembling. The strongest of the soldiers were already gathering brush and breaking up deadfall from the canyon floor and lighting fires. Here, at least, thought McGarry, there was plentiful wood—unlike most places in this godforsaken Great Basin.

The major rode up on a sergeant haranguing a private who was still mounted and sagging in the saddle.

"What's the matter here, Sergeant Robbins?"

"It's Private Collins, sir. He will not dismount."

"What seems to be the problem, trooper?" McGarry said.

The private, barely able to stay upright, did not answer but merely shook his head back and forth.

"Dismount, Private Collins. That's an order!"

Collins was unresponsive.

"Collins!" McGarry yelled, then shoved him hard against the shoulder.

The force of the push sent the limp trooper off the left side of the blaze-faced sorrel horse, and, as his right foot crossed over the seat of the saddle the stirrup came with it. Head and shoulders landed in the trampled snow and the horse snorted and shied, sidestepping away from the odd load that dangled at his side.

"My God!" said Sergeant Robbins.

"What is it?"

"It's his boot, sir," Robbins replied as he grabbed the reins of the alarmed horse. "It's froze fast in the stirrup." The horse kept up snorting and stomping and sidestepping and spinning, slinging the soldier as it went, which added to the horse's panic as did Sergeant Robbins hanging from the headstall, attempting to calm the animal but having the opposite effect.

"Soldier!" McGarry shouted at the nearest trooper. "A little help here!"

The man stumbled over and joined Sergeant Robbins on the horse's head, grabbing the opposite cheek strap and stopping the horse, if not controlling it. Another soldier saw the difficulty and took over for the sergeant, who turned his attention to levering the frozen foot out of the stirrup, which was accomplished with a good deal of tugging and twisting, and the poking and punching away of hunks of packed snow and ice.

With his right foot free, the hung-up trooper rolled onto his back, his left foot still pointing skyward and likewise frozen in its stirrup. Sergeant Robbins freed that one as well, then ordered one of the men to tend to the horse and the other to help drag Private Collins to one of the newly kindled campfires.

McGarry was a good deal more careful of others still mounted, spreading word among the troops to watch out for similar problems and help those who needed it. The situation was worse than he had thought. He rode toward a trooper sitting cross-legged in the snow holding his horse.

"What's the problem, soldier?"

"Feet don't want to work, Major sir," the man mumbled.

McGarry swung off his horse and, as he loosened the strap that held the man's canteen to the saddle, said, "I'll get someone over to help you directly. Meantime, suck on this a bit." Freeing the canteen, McGarry hefted it and gave it a shake. "Hell's bells, Private, it froze!"

McGarry uncorked the canteen to test the contents. Sure enough, most of what was inside was ice and slush. A small sip set McGarry to sputtering, the only thing fluid enough to pour being straight alcohol. He replaced the cap and tossed the canteen at the trooper, and it landed like a brick in his lap.

"Prop that next to the fire for a while when you get to one. Be a damn shame to let good whiskey go to waste just because it's got a few icicles in it," he said, glad that he had had the good sense to keep his flask in his shirt pocket during the march. And the foresight to stow his canteen—two of them, as a matter of fact—under his overcoat.

After all, a man couldn't be expected to be without his whiskey in trying times such as these.

The major spent another couple of hours seeing that the horses were tended to and the men properly organized, with plenty of fires kindled and lots of firewood laid by. Most of the men simply collapsed at first opportunity, some on their blankets and others huddled on the snow. Eating was largely out of the question anyway, the rations frozen in their haversacks, and many mouths still stitched shut by icy beards and mustaches.

Soon, though, even the minimal warmth from open fires in the mouth of the canyon served to rejuvenate the men, and activity grew as the day lengthened. Meals were eaten, whiskey and water drunk, icy limbs massaged, wet clothing dried before the fires.

The men knew the day would be much shorter than the night just past and the one to come. And they knew that tonight would take them up the steep canyon at their backs, and over the divide to make their way down connecting canyons and into Cache Valley.

Tonight's trip would be shorter than last night's—in miles. But no one imagined it would be any less difficult, and the night itself would be just as long. With more than a foot of snow on the level here in the valley, McGarry guessed they would see several feet of it in the mountains. And Cache Valley, considerably higher in elevation than these valleys surrounding the Great Salt Lake, would likely be blanketed with a couple of feet, at least.

Throughout the day, officers moved the men who had gotten the worst of it into a common area, establishing a sort of field hospital in the snow. All told, more than eighty men reported sick. Ice and snow and cold were the cause of practically all the injuries, from frostbitten cheeks and noses to chilblain on ears and fingers. But the most common malady, by far, was frozen feet.

McGarry strolled among the sick troopers.

"What's your name, Private?"

"Becker, sir."

"What's your complaint, Becker?"

"It's my feet, sir."

"Get up."

"Sir?"

"Stand up, Becker. Are you deaf, too?"

The man struggled to his feet.

"Can you walk, boy?"

"I don't know, sir."

"Try."

Becker gingerly walked a few steps in the cold mud, then circled around the fire stiff legged to return to where McGarry waited.

"Looks like you're doing fine, soldier."

"I'm not so sure, sir."

"You can walk, can't you, Becker? I just saw it."

"Yessir. But I don't think I could walk much farther than that."

"Then you should be grateful you're in the cavalry, you goldbricking bastard. You only have to walk far enough to get on your horse. Now, get your gear together and haul your sorry ass back to your outfit."

"Yessir."

McGarry similarly bullied and shamed a few others back to duty. Others he likewise humiliated by demanding they attempt to walk, or by ordering them to unwrap their bandages for his inspection, or by slapping them awake from fitful, fevered sleep before finally deeming them unfit for service. In the end, McGarry reported to Connor that tonight's march and the fight ahead would be short seventy-five men.

"Well, Major," Connor said, "I suppose the rest of us will have that many more Shoshoni to kill. But kill them we will, regardless. Am I clear?"

CHAPTER EIGHTEEN

Tin Dup was old. Eccentric. A lunatic, perhaps.

Tin Dup, and people like him, were beloved among the *Newe,* The People.

Tin Dup was a storyteller. Always, and especially at Warm Dance time, children gathered around Tin Dup to hear him repeat the same stories, over and over, again and again, passing along the history and traditions of the Shoshoni through rote and repetition.

Tin Dup was a mystic. He spent much of his time outside the normal world, visiting places in his mind (or out of it) that no one else could fathom. Oftentimes the old man would talk to the beings of these other worlds, long conversations in strange languages that no one else of the Shoshoni, or any other people, understood.

Tin Dup was an exhorter. He ranted and raved, lectured and criticized. He offered opinions . . . more than opinions—sureties, certainties . . . on every subject and for every eventuality. Sometimes, the leaders of The People listened, and sometimes they did not. Sometimes, they followed the advice, and sometimes they did the opposite. No one kept a tally to determine which was the wiser course. But, in most cases, most people felt their decision might be the wrong one no matter whether their decision went with the old man's advice or against it.

Tin Dup was a dreamer, a seer, a prophet. He saw things in

his sleep and in his mind and behind his eyes, and sometimes the things he saw foreshadowed things that happened later. But sometimes they did not. So people were as ambivalent about the old man's dreams as they were his advice. And, again, when they decided to do or not to do a thing based on a dream of Tin Dup, they always worried the decision might be the wrong one.

Tin Dup, himself, was troubled by this latest dream. Late last night, he had been awakened in the bitter cold by an overfull bladder and had wrapped in a robe and shuffled slowly over the cold, hard ground to the place in the willows away from the camp where people relieved themselves. He could not tell the time because the sky was thick with clouds and snow was falling. Even in the river bottom the wind blew briskly, whipping the snow around until Tin Dup could see nothing of the land around the camp. Even the column of steam over the hot spring was lost in the wind and snow.

He finished his business and hobbled back to the village. No one else was stirring, and the glow from the fires in the lodges was dim, so he knew plenty of time for sleep remained. At his age, Tin Dup required little rest, and when he did doze off his sleep was often fitful and often troubled by dreams. Some he could not remember at all but still awoke anxious and uneasy for having dreamed them. Some dreams were incoherent patchworks of scenes and images that made no sense to him, dreams whose meaning, if any, was indecipherable. Others seemed crystal clear in their content and their interpretation.

Such was the dream of Tin Dup that night after his return to his pallet and robes.

"I saw this village. It was definitely *this* village, but it was not the same as now," Tin Dup told the chiefs, assembled in emergency council at his request. "The snow was not white. Instead, it was all colors. It was brown and yellow, purple and blue. And mostly red."

"What does this colored snow mean?" said Bear Hunter.

"I do not know. Except the red, I think, is blood."

Pocatello said, "Why do you say that?"

"Because of what else I saw. I saw soldiers. Lots of soldiers. They were shooting down the *Newe,* who were helpless. In my dream The People could do nothing to help themselves; they could only look on helplessly as they were shot and beaten and hacked and stabbed and their blood spilled on the snow."

"But why?" Lehi wondered. "Shoshoni would not stand still and be slaughtered. We would fight. We would kill the soldiers."

"I know it," Tin Dup said. "But I do not know why it was not so in my dream. Maybe the fighting men were all dead."

"Then it was not fighting men the soldiers were killing?" said Sagwitch, with both surprise and horror in his voice.

"No. There were some, but mostly I saw the soldiers shooting down our women and old people. And even the children."

"How can such a thing be?" Sagwitch said.

"I do not know. That is all I saw in my dream."

The chiefs sat quietly for a time, huddled around the fire.

Finally, Sanpitch spoke. "Do you think this dream is real, Tin Dup, or did something you ate not agree with you?"

"I cannot say. You know how these dreams are. This one was clearer than most. But I do not know if that means it is more real or not."

"But you have more experience with your dreams than anyone," Bear Hunter said. "What do you think? What do you say?"

"I am afraid. I am old, and tired, and it does not matter if I die. But I am afraid for The People. If this is a true dream, it will be a bad thing. I do not know how it could turn out like this, but there are many things I do not know. I do not know what to tell you."

"But you always have something to say. Sometimes I think

you have too much to say. Why will you not say something now?"

"I do not know. This is different. I am worried. I do not know what to think or say about this dream. If you make me say something, I will say that The People should leave this place."

"No!" Sagwitch said. "You do not even know if this dream is real and yet you want The People to leave this place and tramp off through the storm to find another camp—one that will not be as sheltered and warm as this one!"

Bear Hunter said, "Sagwitch, we cannot have it both ways. We should not ask Tin Dup to say something when he is reluctant to do so and then complain when we do not like what he says."

"But to leave our camp? That is too much."

"I am sorry, Sagwitch," Tin Dup said. "I cannot change the dream."

"But you yourself say you do not know if it is real."

"That is true. I do not know. But I would not want to take a chance. If it is not true, what have we lost by leaving? There are other camps."

Sagwitch stood. "Think of what you are saying, Tin Dup. There are nearly a thousand people here for the Warm Dance. Picking up and moving is no small job in the best of times. And now it is bitter cold and stormy. It is likely that people would die in such a move. Many people."

And then Pocatello spoke up. "Maybe more would die if we stay here. I think Tin Dup is right. The soldiers are angry."

"Yes, they are. They are angry because your young men will not stop stealing and killing," Sagwitch said, sitting once again at his place in the circle.

"The young men will do what they will do. And the soldiers will do what they will do. If they are determined to wipe The People off the face of the Earth then that is what they will try to do, no matter what."

"I would have guessed you would want to fight the soldiers, not run away," Bear Hunter said.

"I will fight them. Unlike Sagwitch, I am not a friend of any of the white men. Not the Mormons, not the Americans, not the soldiers. They are all the same to me, and I will fight them all. But not now. Not here. This is not a good time for a fight. The dream of Tin Dup only sustains my beliefs."

"Sanpitch, what do you think?"

"It is a troubling dream. And we have heard there are soldiers coming."

"You mean the foot soldiers coming from Salt Lake City?" Bear Hunter said. "They are but a few and are only coming to take back a wagon train of wheat. Are those the ones you mean?"

"Those are the ones. But it is not good that they are coming. Maybe it is a trick. And that white man that Pocatello's people killed a few weeks ago down there by Richmond, maybe that has angered the soldiers, and they mean to fight."

Sagwitch said, "There are not enough of them to fight us. If they come, they will want us to give up the killers and return the goods and the stock. That is what they have done before."

"The Mormons do that—but I think the soldiers will not be satisfied with that. We know these soldiers that are here now like to kill The People," Bear Hunter said.

Pocatello said, "If they want the young men who killed that man, they will not get them. And if it is a fight they want, they will not get that from my people, either. For me and my people will be gone when the soldiers get here."

Bear Hunter was surprised at Pocatello's plan. "You are leaving, then? You are taking Tin Dup's advice?"

"Yes. I am leaving, and I will encourage the people who follow me to leave with me. I believe they will come. We will go to our winter camp up the river where those other hot springs are." Pocatello shrugged. "We would be leaving soon anyway.

The Warm Dance is over, and so we will leave now."

"Lehi, what do you think?" Bear Hunter said.

"This is where my band always stays in winter. We will not go with Pocatello to his camp. I do not know about this dream of Tin Dup's soldiers killing us, so we will stay here like always. We will see what happens."

"Sagwitch?"

"I will stay. Here, the Mormons are nearby and will help us if we get too hungry. In some other place, help is a long way away, and I would not know the settlers as well. I feel safer here. My people will stay."

"Sanpitch?"

"We will go with Pocatello. That is our camp, too, sometimes. As Pocatello said, the Warm Dance is over, and it would soon be time to go anyway. I would like to wait for better weather, but I think we had better go now."

Pocatello said, "How about you, Bear Hunter? You are the most respected chief among our people. You have always led us in war. The People will pay more attention to what you say than to any of us."

"I am old, and my influence is waning. The People will do what they want to do, as always. I cannot force them to stay or to go. But, as for me, I intend to stay here."

"What if Tin Dup's dream is true and the soldiers come?"

"Then so be it. I do not want to fight the soldiers. And I do not believe that little band of solders is coming to fight us. Maybe the dream will come true, but maybe not now. Maybe some other time."

"Maybe you are right. But we will go anyway."

"That will be as you wish, Pocatello. But hear this: if the soldiers come and if, as Sagwitch says, they want to arrest the killers of that man, we will tell the soldiers that the killers are not from this camp and not from these people but belong to a band that is no longer here. So, do not be surprised if the soldiers leave us alone and come looking for you."

Pocatello and Sanpitch did not waste any time in getting their people packed up and on the trail. Many grumbled about traveling in the snow and wind and cold, and some stayed despite the fears of their leaders. Others of Bear Hunter's and Sagwitch's and Lehi's bands had heard of Tin Dup's dream and were afraid and followed Pocatello.

By the time the sun was high in the sky—or would have been, had there been any sunshine in the heavy, cold clouds—more than half the people in the village under the bluffs where Beaver Creek meets the *Boa Ogoi* were gone.

Still, seventy-five lodges and some four hundred people waited to see if the dream of Tin Dup would come true.

CHAPTER NINETEEN

The cove at the canyon's mouth just east of the Mormon burg called Brigham City provided some protection from the wind, Rockwell thought. At least a man could walk upright without fear of being upended by the gale. As he tended to his horse, the cavalry troopers tucked into the recess, recuperating from last night's long, hard ride. Fires burned for warmth, but no cooking fires blazed because the troops had eaten cold meals carried from Camp Douglas in haversacks—which food they were only able to chew after it had been exposed to the fires long enough to thaw.

Strategy dictated the troops lay low here until nightfall, then push on through the canyon and into Cache Valley under cover of darkness.

In the low afternoon light, Colonel Connor crossed the bivouac to where the horses were picketed, looking for Porter Rockwell. He found his scout hunched over next to his mount with the horse's right foreleg tucked between his knees, working the sole of the hoof over with a hoof pick.

"You appear to be a man who takes care of his horses, Mister Rockwell."

Rockwell finished with the hoof and lowered it to the ground, stood upright, and patted the horse's neck before answering.

"I learned long ago that a man in my line of work needs a sound horse between his knees. He soon enough ends up dead if he don't."

114

"And what line of work would that be? I have heard tell of your involvement in any number of endeavors."

"Have you, now? Well, most likely it ain't but half true. Leastways, that's how it is with most of what I've heard told about me."

"So tell me the half that is true."

Rockwell hefted the horse's off hind leg, propped it on his thigh, and put the hoof pick back to work. "I don't guess I've done much you'd find interesting. Some lawman type stuff— tracking down horse and cattle thieves and other scofflaws and criminals and such. Guarding folks, and property; stagecoaches and wagon trains and mail shipments and the like. Recovering stolen stock. Lately, been doin' some ranching. Some cattle; mostly horses. Been partners in keeping a roadside hotel and hospitality joint down at the Point of the Mountain these last few years, too."

"So, you would say your reputation as a killer is undeserved."

Allowing the horse's hoof to drop, Rockwell patted the animal on the hip, then pulled his mittens from the pocket of his coat and tugged them over his hands. "Let's get next to a fire, Colonel. The cold is catching up to me out here." He set off for the camp with Connor at his side.

"So, what do you say, Rockwell?"

"Oh, I've been in a few shooting scrapes. Had to protect myself, or someone in my charge, from time to time. Some prisoners or fugitives try to escape and need to be stopped. You know how it goes."

"Those who describe you as a cold-blooded murderer and assassin are mistaken, then?"

Rockwell cast a hard look at the colonel and considered his answer. "Mister Connor, I ain't never killed no one that didn't need killing."

Connor found no reply.

"Now, can I ask you a question?"

Connor nodded.

"This Major McGarry. I get the feeling he'd as soon shit in my dinner plate as look at me. What'd I ever do to him?"

With a short snort of a laugh, Connor said, "Hard to say, Rockwell. I suspect he does not approve of your reputation. And, unlike myself, he is willing to accept what he hears without hesitation."

That drew a laugh from Rockwell. "I have heard a few things about the major, as far as that goes."

The men were now back at the campground, rapidly being disassembled as the sun dropped through breaking clouds to fall ever nearer the mountains far to the southwest and across the Great Salt Lake. Connor's fire would be smothered last, after the officers had assembled for orders for the night's march through the mountains. The colonel found a seat on a fallen log dragged next to the fire for that purpose and invited Rockwell to sit beside him.

"So, what do you know of my Major McGarry, Rockwell?" Connor said as he peeled off his mittens and extended the palms of his hands toward the blaze.

Rather than sitting beside Connor, Rockwell plopped down on an upright saw log. He, too, removed his mittens, stuffed them in his coat pockets, then rubbed the palms of his small hands together briskly. "That he's a hothead," he said. "Mistreats his men and his horses. I can't abide a man who abuses a horse. He's said to be a drunk, and a mean one at that."

"I will say only that much of the major's reputation is deserved."

"They say he's killed Indians when it wasn't necessary. Hell, I had the reports read to me right out of the newspapers. Very likely McGarry himself is the cause of the problem you're wanting to solve with this little war you've declared."

"That may be true, Rockwell. It may very well be true."

"So tell me this, Mister Connor. Why's he along? Why's he in charge of the cavalry troops? Better still, why's a mean bastard like him still in the army?"

"Very simple. He pitches in, Rockwell. Major McGarry is a man of action, albeit occasionally misguided. All things being equal, there will always be a place in my command for a man who will fight. So it will be necessary for you to abide the major, no matter your feelings about his treatment of horses. Am I clear?"

Rockwell nodded.

"Now, Mister Rockwell, it is time I assembled the officers and staff to convey orders. So, tell me, what might we expect tonight? What about these canyons?"

"It won't be no Sunday school picnic, for sure. We'll be sheltered some of the time from the worst of the wind, but there'll be more snow. Three or four feet, likely, up on the divide."

"But don't other travelers to Cache Valley keep the road packed? I assume there is regular traffic to and from the settlements there?"

"There is, some. But with the fresh snow, and even more so on account of these winds, what road there is will be drifted over so's you won't even know it was there. We'll make her through, though."

Connor considered Rockwell's report for a time before saying, "Perhaps we should have taken the other route into the valley—the one followed by the infantry and supply wagons."

Rockwell sniffed. "Well, them boys afoot with their wagons likely had an easier time of it—if they beat the storm. But that road ain't so easy either in bad weather. 'Sides, up that way you'd be more likely to be seen by some Shoshoni or other, out hunting or something."

Connor nodded understanding, then unfurled what served as maps. Hunched over the crude sketches, the scout and the colonel studied where the track leading them to the Shoshoni should best be laid. Once through the canyon, Rockwell told Connor, they would reach Wellsville. It was the first of the Mormon settlements in the Valley, plopped down on the first piece of level ground coming down from the canyon. From there, there were options to consider.

The main road left Wellsville to veer toward the east side of the valley to strike Providence, then follow to the north near the base of the Bear River mountains to Logan, Smithfield, Richmond, and, finally, Franklin—the northernmost of the Cache Valley settlements. Rockwell recommended another route.

"If we bear a bit toward the west out of Wellsville and follow the Little Bear River downstream, we'll come to this little town called Mendon," Rockwell said, stabbing at a spot on the map. "It's off in the west side of the valley by itself, so we'll attract less notice. And, unless I miss my guess, that's where your wagons will be—leastways somewhere near there."

Rockwell's finger moved about the map. "A ways north of that town, the Little Bear meets the Bear. From there, you just follow the main river upstream. You could follow it all the way to where I reckon the Shoshoni camp is if you wanted to. But I guess you'll be wanting to send your foot soldiers and wagons a ways east, to where the Cub River comes in. Give 'em a good head start and meet up with them outside of Franklin."

"What about these rivers," Connor said, pointing out several squiggly lines. "Will there be trouble in the crossing?"

"Nah. Give a man a minute to work on a chaw of tobacco, and he could spit clean across them all, save the Bear."

Connor counted that as at least one entry on the plus side of the balance sheet for the expedition.

CHAPTER TWENTY

And the first shall be last.

Geese breaking trail at the thin edge of a migrating wedge will tire, drop off the lead, and take up a position in the rear. That is the way the California Volunteers crossed the mountains.

Eastward up the narrow defile of Box Elder Canyon, through a foot, then foot and a half of snow, the column faced little difficulty. The lead four plowed through the powdery snow, trampled in turn by the hundreds of following hoofs into a hard-packed road.

But by the time they reached the little mountain valley called Box Elder and veered northward, the depth of the snow would grow and progress slow. The long climb to the summit, nearly five thousand and nine hundred feet in the night sky, would bring ever deeper snow with every step.

Two feet. Then three. Four, finally. No job for a horse, this. Dismounted men broke a narrow trail for their animals, and the path widened in their wake, stretching out behind in the successive tracks of ever more horses.

The winds and snows of the storms of last night and yesterday served to erase any trace of a road. The passage of the cavalry toward Cache Valley and the supply wagons with rations for men and mounts was a matter of faith.

But Rockwell knew the way and assured Connor and the questioning officers that the path he pointed out between ridges and through draws and over rises would lead the expedition through the mountains and into the valley.

Over the divide, then down the hill and across the bowl where Dry Lake comes and goes with the spring, the snow did not diminish. Then, out of the hole and over the broad saddle, and along the long ridge to turn a hard right around the wheel of Cart Hill the troopers struggled, at last finding a bit of relief in the protective gorge of Wellsville Canyon as it drops eastward, leaving the deepest snow behind.

Then the canyon's jaws widen and the road—both the hidden road and the road the troopers made in its place—veers to follow the needle of the compass toward the north. The town at the mouth of the canyon was felt and smelled and heard more than seen, as daylight was yet to reach Cache Valley. But Wellsville was there, behind a curtain of stove smoke from banked fires. Barking dogs and the whinny of corralled horses announced their arrival as the cavalry column skirted the village to ride on and drop into the bottomland along Little Bear River to rest man and animal.

Soon, smoke from campfires hung in the cold air, mingling with that from the stoves and fireplaces of Wellsville, filtering an already weak rising sun.

And in the barnyards of the awakening town, warm milk would ring the bottoms of metal pails and turn to steam and foam as stanchioned cows chewed mouthfuls of grain, grinding in synch with the jawbones of a hundred and a half cavalry horses, up to their eyes in nose bags in the woods by the river beneath the shallow butte.

CHAPTER TWENTY-ONE

The valley and town of Tooele in Utah Territory are a far, far distance from Cache Valley. In a direct line measured in miles, one hundred. By any other measure, half a world away.

Hear Mary Ann Weston Maughan's first impression of Cache Valley: "When we got to the mouth of the Canyon, we stopped to look at the Beautiful Valley before us my first words were O What a beautiful Valley."

The dominant color of Cache Valley in season is green. The words *lush,* and *fertile,* and *verdant,* and *luxuriant* appear often in descriptions of the place. A welcome sight for Mary Ann Weston Maughan and her husband, Peter, and their children, refugees from the Tooele Valley, where none of those words applies.

The western edge of the Salt Lake Valley is confined by the Oquirrh Mountains, and that range also defines the eastern edge of the Tooele Valley. From any point of view along the western slope of the Oquirrhs, until one's vision is halted by the Stansbury Mountains—which define the western bounds of the Tooele Valley—shades of drab are dominant to the point of near exclusivity. Drab hues of brown. Tan. Ochre. Gray. Sepia. Ash. Bronze. Buff. Umber. Olive. Amber. Beige. All and every one, drab.

The dirt is drab. The rocks are drab. The grass is drab. The brush is drab. Even in the trees, which are so rare as to be remarkable, the green is so shabby and worn and powdered with earth that only drab shows through. The things you see that are not drab in their natural state—the manmade things—take on a drab tinge from drab dust that precipitates out of the drab dirt and drab rocks and drab grass and drab brush to settle on the surface of every windblown thing. So, it is not difficult to understand Sister Maughan's delight in her new home.

The community they founded there, first called Maughan's Fort, then Wellsville, followed the established pattern of Mormon settlement, a pattern established by Brigham Young and repeated in every habitable place available as converts to the Church of Jesus Christ of Latter-day Saints gathered to their Zion to fill those settlements.

Contrary to the norm on the frontier, the Mormon way of settlement spurned the isolated homestead and the remote ranch. Rather, the Saints, instead, huddled settlers in compact villages.

The warp of the pattern was the economic design of the Mormon faith: each family received a town lot, as much arable land on the outskirts of town as the family could farm profitably for their own sustenance and that of the community, and grazing rights in the communal pastures that ringed the cultivated ground.

The weft of the pattern was protection. Brigham Young encouraged Cache Valley settlers—as in other settlements—to live "close together, then, if you are disturbed, you are like a hive of bees, and everyone is ready and knows at once what to do."

But contrast the beauty of Cache Valley in spring and summer and fall with its long, stark winters. In the years prior to settlement, pioneers tried the place as a herding ground for cattle. Snow fell early on the experiment, and cowboys attempted to round up the two thousand Mormon cattle and drive them through the snowbound canyon to more hospitable terrain. A few more than four hundred head survived.

Brigham remembered and gave with his permission to settle a warning: "You are perfectly aware, Brother Maughan, that you at that place are perfectly cut off from any of our settlements during the winter." And, he counseled, "You must be very cautious about the hostile Indians from the north."

Needing no instruction in the violent nature of Cache Valley winters, based on his few hours' and days' personal experience, it was the hostility of the Indians Porter Rockwell inquired about when he knocked on Peter Maughan's door.

"Brother Maughan?"

"Yes. And that is Porter Rockwell under that bundle of clothes unless I am mistaken. How is it with you?"

"Wheat. All wheat."

The odd expression was a favorite of Rockwell's, and one familiar to all who had dealings with him. It derived from the biblical metaphor of separating the wheat from the tares, the bad from the good, the wheat being the good. So, Rockwell used the word to cover any favorable eventuality that was fine, good, well, acceptable, and the like.

"It has been a long time, Brother Rockwell. Come in out of the cold. I would offer you coffee, but our supply is spent. Hot Brigham tea, perhaps?"

"No, but thank you. Coffee is one thing I have had enough of traveling with the soldier boys. I have requisitioned a small supply of the stuff to replenish your stores," Rockwell said as he peeled off his long buffalo-robe coat and fetched a bundle from the pocket of his canvas coat, handing the package to Maughan, who took it with an appreciative smile. "I don't suppose our army slipped by you unnoticed, Brother Maughan."

"We have begged federal officials for soldiers for a long time without result. And now hardly a day goes by, it seems, that a contingent is not seen in the valley," Maughan said with a chuckle. "Even now, a small encampment of soldiers and freight wagons has been seen up near Mendon."

"The foot soldiers were supposed to be seen. But if a Shoshoni should ask, I hope you will deny the presence of the cavalry hiding down there in the river bottom. The army intends to inform them of our arrival by surprise."

"We have not seen Indians at this end of the valley for some weeks. But you will find a passel of them up north."

"I'll want to know about that. But first, I wonder if you'll satisfy my curiosity about what led up to all this. Brother Brigham didn't tell me much, but he said you'd kept him on top of things here."

"It is true. President Young and I have corresponded freely since we came back to our valley in '59 after the evacuation for the Utah War. You want me to go back that far?"

"I hear there was a big set-to last fall. Start there."

Ever a talkative sort, Peter Maughan could not resist the opportunity to spin a tale. So he backed into the story with a preamble. "That I will. But I'll have to back up a bit to get there. You see, relationships with the Lamanites are generally favorable so long as we can afford to supply them with wheat and flour and vegetables in summer, and a few cattle from time to time. Still, they are always prone to steal horses.

"But, to get to the story, three summers ago a fellow up Smithfield way felt threatened and shot and killed a Shoshoni called Pagunap, who was chief of a small band. His people killed two of the Saints in return. Those killed had nothing to do with it. The Indians are happy to kill the first person they find for revenge, rather than seeking out the guilty party.

"Anyway, that marks the beginning of the present difficulties, and there have been numerous little fights. One of the Shoshoni's big chiefs, Sagwitch, has kept his people somewhat in hand by demanding and getting more provisions than we can afford to give. It has been a grievous tax to be borne, I will tell you.

"Now, to last summer. Over a three-week stretch, the Indians made off with a hundred horses from around the valley. Since we had just given them tons of flour and beef, we were most displeased. They had been acting bold and saucy, too, coming into our houses and insulting the women and such. We sent a group of our Minute Men out to recover the stock, but even with help from friendly Indians we only brought back ten head.

"The mess you are referring to, I suspect, happened later— November it was, and really had naught to do with us. That one started when a fellow named Van Ornum, Zachius Van Ornum as I recall, showed up here with a troop of cavalry."

"Was this Van Ornum a soldier?"

"Civilian. Which made us wonder, I can tell you. We couldn't get any cooperation from the United States government no matter what we did, and here this man shows up with soldiers in tow. Well, the story goes that this man's brother had been killed in a fight away out west on the Oregon Trail a couple of years earlier. Most everyone in the outfit was killed, save three girls and a young boy, who the Indians took away. The girls died, he said, but he kept hearing stories about a white boy among the Indians, and one of those stories put the boy here in Cache Valley with Bear Hunter's people.

"So, this Van Ornum made his way to Salt Lake City, and he convinced the commander of the soldiers at that new camp of theirs down there to help him rescue the lad. The cavalry officer he sent was a man named McGarry. A lower sort of human I do not believe I have ever met. He was profane, blasphemous, belligerent, and a drunkard. Anyway, they located Bear Hunter's band camped on the bench above Providence and attacked without warning—McGarry did not even bother to state his business, just started shooting.

"The Shoshoni scrambled up a little canyon to the east and

started shooting back. Bear Hunter—he's a smart one—laid out their defenses so the soldiers couldn't make any headway. They traded gunfire for a couple of hours without result until the old chief tired of the game. He rode out with a few of his braves to meet the army under a flag of truce.

"That lowborn McGarry, though, he did not honor the truce and seized Bear Hunter and a few others and threatened to kill them if the Shoshoni did not produce the boy. The boy was not there, though. He had gone away with his mother and some others a few days before. McGarry told the Indians to find him and that he would hold their chief and the others hostage until he got the boy but would kill them if he did not get him.

"Next day, they brought in the boy. He was blond, all right, and had blue eyes. But that boy was Shoshoni through and through. Didn't speak nor understand a word of English. He did not want to go with Van Ornum and the soldiers and scratched and clawed like a wildcat. But McGarry took him anyway. The Shoshoni knew he wasn't the Van Ornum boy at all. Seems he was the son of a French trapper and one of Chief Washakie's sisters from over Wind River way."

By now, Rockwell was nervous from sitting so long in the warm kitchen and started pacing the room.

"Old Bear Hunter was not happy about the whole situation, I can tell you," Maughan continued, barely pausing for breath. "He rode into Providence the next day with his warriors, threatening the Saints and accusing them of cowardice for not fighting the soldiers with him. Several dozens of our Minute Men rode down from Logan to deal with the saucy Indians but instead bought off further trouble with a couple of beeves and a load of flour."

Maughan then told Rockwell the version of the story prevalent in Cache Valley of McGarry's killing of bound Shoshoni captives at Empey's Ferry, over the mountain in early

December, shortly after his foray into Providence. It was the opinion of most, Maughan told Rockwell, that those executions had served no other purpose than to further enrage the Indians. And, indeed, Maughan related an incident that happened a month after the killings, in which the Shoshoni robbed and tormented a group of miners traveling from Montana to Salt Lake City, finally murdering one of the men near Richmond.

"Word is, Bear Hunter intends to kill white men until he feels satisfied his people have been avenged for the men McGarry had shot at the ferry. He told me himself, after the skirmish at Providence, that he would kill the next soldiers he saw and said he would welcome them back anytime for a fight. It seems, Brother Rockwell, the army has taken up the challenge."

Rockwell thought over Maughan's stories, then said, "Colonel Connor has made it plain that he intends to do some Indian killing. But I believe he'd as soon get it done without any fighting—catch them unawares and shoot them down before there's much danger to his soldiers." After another pause for thought, he talked on. "You said the Shoshoni were up north. We hear tell they usually winter at a place near Franklin. Is that right?"

"It is. You will find hundreds of them camped in the river bottoms ten, maybe twelve miles north and a bit west of the town. The bishop in Franklin, Preston Thomas, gives them flour when he can. The other settlements in the valley supply the bishop, so we share the load. Which has been a big load this past month, I tell you. There seem to be more Shoshoni there than just Bear Hunter's bands. I do not know why."

"What can you tell me of the lay of the land thereabouts, and the layout of the camp?"

"Nothing, I am afraid. I have ridden through the area but do not know it well enough to tell you what you need to know. I suggest when you get to Franklin you talk to Ed or Joe Nelson. They have visited the camp and know the area. If they are reluctant, do not hesitate to invoke my name. As stake president over the Cache Valley, I trust I still have some influence."

"Thank you, Brother Maughan. It is good to see you again after all these years. Tell me, do you miss Tooele?"

"I once had a carbuncle, Brother Rockwell. Terribly painful and a tremendous nuisance. The relief that came with its healing is the only thing I can think of to compare with our feelings upon leaving that place. And you?"

"Oh, I get through there from time to time. I still run stock on beyond there in Rush Valley. And I've lately taken up another ranch even farther out, on Government Creek. But I do not mind the isolation as some do," Rockwell said as he pulled on his heavy coat and left the house. A few steps into the dooryard he turned back for a final word with Peter Maughan.

"By the way, your old friend Major McGarry commands the cavalry yonder," Rockwell said, inclining his head in the direction of the troops. "Shall I give him your best?"

"By all means. I wish the soldiers every success. But, as for McGarry himself, you can tell him I hope his hair ends up ornamenting Bear Hunter's lance."

CHAPTER TWENTY-TWO

The room was hot and stuffy from too big a fire in the stove, and glaringly bright from too many lit lanterns. As usual in such circumstances, Porter Rockwell felt confined. His nerves were on edge, and the timidity about cooperating he found among the leaders of the town of Franklin did nothing to soothe his troubled mind.

Once he had successfully guided Colonel Connor and Major McGarry and the cavalry companies to their appointment with the infantry and saw them safely encamped in an out of the way place between Mendon and Franklin, Rockwell had ridden on to Franklin to learn what he could and to ask the town to stand by with any help that might be needed.

But the leaders were reluctant to lend assistance. In the room with him were the local bishop, Preston Thomas, his counselor and the operator of the local cooperative mercantile, William Hull, and the brothers Ed and Joe Nelson, recommended by Peter Maughan back in Wellsville as local guides.

"How do we know this won't be like them soldiers' last two escapades in these parts?" asked William Hull.

"Brother Hull has a point, Rockwell," Bishop Thomas said. "All the army has managed to accomplish thus far is to anger the Shoshoni. They've taken their blood revenge against travelers on the road thus far, but sooner or later it's bound to be us."

The "soldiers' escapades" the men referred to were Major

129

McGarry's December killing of four hostages at Empey's Ferry and the seizure of Bear Hunter during the mission to rescue the Van Ornum boy. The Shoshoni response had been an increase in stock rustling and the harassment and robbery of wayfarers on the Montana road, including the killing of one of a party of miners, which breach of the peace was behind the army's presence in the valley. And, the reason for Rockwell's presence in this room.

"It's been a matter of bad manners and stolen livestock and demands for more food from us up till now," Thomas said. "We haven't had a settler killed in more than two years. How do we know that won't change if the Shoshoni are further angered?"

"If Colonel Connor pulls this thing off as planned, you won't have to worry about angry Indians," Rockwell said.

"And why is that?" Hull said.

"Because they'll all be dead."

The men were visibly taken aback.

After taking a moment to find his voice, Thomas said, "All of them, Rockwell? Surely the soldiers will seize and punish the guilty parties. But do they really intend to wipe out the entire band?"

"That's the army's usual way of doing things. Leastways, Connor's way of dealing with Indians."

"But that just ain't right!" Hull said.

"For hell's sake! You people up here have been whining to the church for years about having to feed the Indians and complaining that the government ain't no help. Well, here they are to help, and now you don't want it?"

"It's not the kind of help we want, Rockwell," Bishop Thomas said.

"I see. You bellyache that you don't get no help, and now you bellyache about the kind of help you're getting. I was always told not to look a gift horse in the mouth."

The men sat again in silence for a time, digesting what had been said and working up the appetite to continue the conversation. It was William Hull who finally broke the silence.

"Brother Rockwell, among my other jobs here, I run the Bishop's Storehouse and the co-op. Over the past two, three years I've loaded more sacks of flour and wheat than I can count onto Indian ponies. They've hauled away a goodly portion of our garden produce and whatever else we've managed to harvest. And I've seen more head of donated cattle than I can even remember driven off by the Shoshoni.

"I'm willing to say I didn't think feeding them was a good plan, at least not always. But it was the plan the Lord give to us—at least that's what I was told by Peter Maughan, who said them was the orders from Salt Lake, and we was to abide by them. So, I went along. We was to keep the Indians on our side and avoid fighting with them.

"Seems to me all that food was wasted if all it bought us was a little time. I'd have been happy to start shooting them thieving Shoshoni long ago if I'd a known it was coming to that anyway."

"Brother Hull puts it in different terms than I would, Brother Rockwell, but it still ends up in the same place," Bishop Thomas said. "The church's practice with our Lamanite brethren has always been to feed them rather to fight them. If we are to believe you, that has changed."

"I ain't fit to talk of such things, Bishop. What the church does and don't do ain't up to me."

"And yet you are asking us to disregard all previous advice to pacify the Indians and instead stand by and see them slaughtered. Even participate, to a degree," Thomas said. "I question your authority to demand such a radical change."

"Unless he steered me wrong, Peter Maughan is still stake president in these parts. He said you'd cooperate on his say-so.

And I'll remind you that Brigham Young told me—told me himself, right in his office—that I was to come along on this little adventure with Colonel Connor. So I guess the authority in question ain't mine. I'm asking on the say-so of President Maughan and Brother Brigham himself. It's crude to put it this way, Bishop, but you're outranked. And it ain't by me."

The stove continued to put out more heat than was needed. Too many lanterns continued to shine brighter than necessary. And Rockwell continued to fidget in the close room as the Franklin men stayed quiet with their thoughts, chewing over something that seemed simple and straightforward to him. Hull and Thomas sat behind a table that served as a desk, Hull's chair leaned back and propped against the wall. The bishop's elbows were propped on his desk, head down in his hands and lost in thought, or maybe prayer.

From his seat off to the side, Rockwell bounced his knee and worried his hat as he watched them, and the two Nelsons, who had sat silent as stone throughout most of the discussion, across the desk from their bishop. It was to the brothers that Rockwell next spoke.

"I reckon you boys are the ones with the help I need the most of, just now. What've you got to say about it?"

"You're wanting one or the other of us to show you the lay of the land between here and the Shoshoni camp on Beaver Creek and nothing more, am I right?" the one called Joe said. At least Rockwell thought it was Joe.

"That's the most of it. I want to be where I can see the camp without being noticed, or at least without looking suspicious. And I'd appreciate anything you can tell me about how them Indians are arranged in the camp so's Connor and them other officers can figure where the soft spots might be. I'm told you boys have been in the camp and might know such things."

This time it was the other Nelson, Ed—at least Rockwell

thought it was Ed—who responded. "We have been there, all right. And that's why I'm a bit uncomfortable with this whole notion. See, me and Joe have known Bear Hunter and Sagwitch and lots of others in that camp for a good long time. They trust us. We'd be betraying that trust, seems to me."

"Ed's right," Joe said. "Without us knowing them, and them trusting us, things would have been a lot worse around here. We've been able to talk to them and keep things calmed down some."

Rockwell snorted. "All I'm asking is for you to show me the place and tell me what you can. If they see me riding around out there, they might think something's up. They might think that anyway. But they're used to seeing you boys and your horses around.

"I ain't no greenhorn at this kind of thing and I could go on about my business with no help from you, and it'd all be wheat. But you could save me considerable time and trouble. And maybe keep me from stumbling into something unhealthy."

"Bishop?" Joe said.

Thomas sat upright and pressed his fingertips against his closed eyelids and rubbed.

"I don't see how you can do otherwise than what the man asks, Brother Nelson. This situation isn't to my liking either, but if the brethren down south want us to cooperate, I suppose we must."

"One more thing, Rockwell," Ed said.

Rockwell gave the man his attention.

"What's in it for us?"

"Nothing I can think of. Knowing you've done your duty, maybe. Or maybe that don't count for much with you."

"I guess it'll have to do."

"But?" Rockwell said, sensing there was more.

"Even Judas got his thirty pieces of silver."

CHAPTER TWENTY-THREE

Six mud-smeared, shaggy-coated horses stood in the street in Franklin in front of the Tithing Office, heads down and backs humped against the cold. Three were saddled in the Shoshoni style; on the others were cinched pack saddles. One of the packhorses was already laden with two heavy sacks, a bushel and a half of wheat in each. One such sack burdened a second horse.

From inside the building came the rhythmic ring of a square-mouthed scoop shovel sliding into wheat piled in the bin, followed by the sibilant slide of the kernels off the broad face of shovel and into a gunnysack.

Squatting low to the ground and propped against the wall of the building sat three Shoshoni men, young men, huddled in their blankets and watching the few comings and goings in the icy streets of the town. The day's light was dimming, the hidden sun low in the southwest behind the thick curtain of cold, pewter-colored clouds.

From somewhere south of town, the sound of wagons and drumming feet carried on the cold wind, and the bundled Shoshoni heard it between the shovel strokes. After a time, coming up the final rise into the town, came Infantry Company K in the uniform of the California Volunteers, followed by steaming horses drawing army supply wagons.

The shoveling stopped, and after a moment Bill Hull, operator of the Tithing Office, came out the door with the newly filled and tied wheat sack on his shoulder. He transferred the load to the second packhorse and as he lashed it down joked, "Here come the *Toquashes*. Maybe you will all be killed."

"Maybe *Toquashes* will be killed, too," one of the Shoshoni replied.

Hull laughed as he secured the knots, then returned to the building and took up his shovel. But when he came out a few minutes later with another sack bulging with wheat, the Shoshoni and all their horses were gone. *The sight of those soldiers must have put the fear of God in them,* Hull thought, *for them to leave without all the promised wheat.* Bishop Preston Thomas had instructed him to give out nine bushels, and the Shoshoni had ridden off leaving three behind. *Well, I suppose they'll be back to collect in a day or two. Or maybe not.*

Carrying the sack back into the granary, Hull dropped it to the floor, picked up a broom, and swept scattered kernels of wheat back into the pile. He hung the broom from its peg, leaned the scoop shovel against the wall, and fixed the lock on the door. Lifting and tucking the collar of his coat high around his neck, he watched the soldiers file past, followed by the squeak and rattle of harnesses and trace chains and singletrees as the teams and wagons rolled past. *They'll wish them wagons was on runners, 'stead of wheels, once they clear the town.* Hull gave his coat collar another tug, thrust his hands into the pockets of his coat, pulled his hat low, ducked his head, and started for home.

Well out of town by now, with arms stretched wide between reins in one hand and lead ropes of reluctant packhorses laden with wheat in the other, the Shoshoni men urged the horses through the graying day. They, and all the people of Bear Hunter's band, had heard that soldiers were on the way to Cache Valley, and the men thought it best to confirm the rumor without delay. The remaining wheat, abandoned at the Mormon

Tithing Office, could be reclaimed later.

It was dark by the time they got back. They struck the river a few miles south of the village, forded at the place where the white man's new road crossed the *Boa Ogoi,* and whipped their tired mounts and dragged the reluctant packhorses across the bottomland in a final dash to the village. The winded horses stood trembling, heads hung low and gasping for air, as the young men relayed the news of the soldiers' arrival.

By the time the chiefs were assembled, word of the *Toquashes* was already flying through the camp. People gathered in small groups, debating the meaning of this development, and arguing over the proper response. Some urged calm and a wait-and-see attitude. Others promoted a fight, even to the point of marching out to meet the soldiers. Some grumbled about the ineptitude of their leaders, while praising the foresight of Pocatello and Sanpitch in quitting the country.

"The soldiers are here! We saw them come to Franklin."

Bear Hunter said, "How many are they?"

"Seventy, I would say. Maybe eighty. They have a few wagons. Not as many as we were told."

"But they are afoot? They are not mounted soldiers?"

"No horses, except for the wagons."

"Maybe what we heard is true," Sagwitch said. "They have come for a shipment of grain."

"It does not seem to me," said Bear Hunter, "that so few would come if they meant to fight."

"But the Tithing Office man, that man Hull, he said that maybe the *Toquashes* would kill us all," said one of the young men.

"He was only joking, I think," said another.

"Even white men would not be stupid enough to attack a village as big as this with so few soldiers," Bear Hunter said. "Still,

I am suspicious. I do not think they are here just for guard duty."

"Maybe they will come to arrest the men who killed that man down by Richmond," Sagwitch said. "They will not believe us when we say they are not here. Or maybe they have come to recover stolen stock. Then, too, they will want to arrest someone."

"Maybe you are right. But what if we do not give up anybody?"

"Maybe then they will want to fight," Lehi said. "Then we can kill them all."

"Yes. And maybe they will kill some of us, too," Bear Hunter said.

"I say it is worth the risk. We may never have a better chance to kill the soldiers. If we kill these, now, maybe all the rest of them will go back where they came from. Maybe they will never come back. Maybe they will go and leave us alone," Lehi said.

"I do not think the soldiers will go away," Bear Hunter said. "If we kill the ones who are here, then more will come to avenge them. And if we kill them, still more will come. One thing I have learned about the whites—there is no end to them."

"I still say we fight. Sooner or later, we are going to have to fight them. And here is a chance to kill some of them before they can kill us."

"Perhaps, Lehi. Perhaps. Sagwitch, what do you think we should do?"

"I think we should wait. If they are here for hauling wheat, then they will leave us alone. If they have come to arrest some of us, we will talk to them and see what can be arranged. If they have come to fight, then we will have to fight them. But it is better not to start a fight we may not be able to finish."

"What do you mean?" Lehi said. "If we cannot whip seventy foot soldiers in a fight, then we deserve to die. Because if it is so that we die so easily, then we have become a village of old women."

"It is as Bear Hunter said—more will come, and then more. So, I say, we fight only if we have to, and that we do not start the fight," Sagwitch said.

Bear Hunter mulled over the thoughts of the other chiefs. He wished he knew more about the intentions of the soldiers. He decided to follow Sagwitch's advice and take a cautious approach. At the same time, he encouraged his people to start melting down lead and molding bullets and to keep the work going into the night so that, if fighting came, the Shoshoni would have as much ammunition as possible. Bear Hunter knew it would not be much—and maybe not enough.

CHAPTER TWENTY-FOUR

29 January 1863

The first snow to fall in a Cache Valley winter is often the last to melt in spring. Cold temperatures and high altitude and a weak sun pull up a snowy quilt and keep the valley tucked in for months.

On the warmest days, the surface of the snow will liquefy, then freeze in the night to form an icy crust that is soon buried under a fresh layer of fallen snow, which will form a crust of its own to be buried in turn in the next storm.

Sometimes, a layer will hold a man, or maybe a horse, or even a wagon for an interval. More often, the crust will fracture under the weight, and the foot or the hoof or the wheel will break through to fall to the next layer of crust, and the next, and so on until travel becomes travail.

The settlers in Cache Valley soon learned—as all people in such circumstances likewise learn—to pull the wheels from the wagons once the snow comes to stay and replace them with runners that distribute the weight over a wider area and glide across the snow rather than trying to bull their way through like the wheels would do.

Captain Sam Hoyt would have done well to have had those lessons. Had he known, his baggage wagons and other conveyances could have crossed the divide and traversed the valley by horsepower alone, without assistance from lifting, prying, pushing, pulling manpower.

And, once they left the road upon leaving the village of Franklin, they might have made it cross country with their wagons and their supplies and camp equipment and ammunition. And the ferocious firepower of the howitzers hidden in the wagon boxes.

Instead, Porter Rockwell, returning from his reconnaissance, rode up on a tumultuous scene of chaos and confusion. He sat watching for a few minutes, hands stacked on the saddle horn, a smile toying with the corners of his mouth.

The line of wagons was farther apart in its spacing than called for in military precision. Each was stalled at the place where the weight of the wagon and the law of gravity overcame the snow and crusty ice, the wheels cutting and dropping until burying the axles and hubs and reaches and hounds and bolsters in the snow until the wagons could no longer move. No amount of whiplash on horses' backs, no amount of hollering of "hup!" and "walk up!" and "pull, you sonsofbitches!" could aid the teams in moving the wagons. They were stuck.

Captain Hoyt cartwheeled through the chaos, ordering infantry soldiers to put shoulders and backs and arms and legs and feet to work to lift and push and pull the wagons free. The men broke out shovels and every other implement even slightly suitable for digging, and snow flew over bent backs and hunched shoulders.

Into the commotion rode Colonel Patrick Edward Connor and Major Edward F. McGarry, in advance of the cavalry. The officers reined up, much as Rockwell had done, and tried to make sense of what they saw. Connor saw Rockwell across the way, shook his head in resignation, and, with the major, made their way to the scout.

"Hell of a mess, Mister Rockwell," Connor said.

Rockwell only nodded in response.

"We will have it sorted out posthaste. What have you learned of savages?"

Rockwell told what he knew. Had there been enough light, he said, he would have been skylighted where he sat horseback on the top of a high bluff above the Bear River. He had stared long and hard down into the river bottom, willing geography out of the darkness.

Dark it was, but not altogether. Cold, dim light, not wholly visible yet present, radiated from the snow-covered ground below. The river's course was a darker line in the darkness. And, across the flood plain against the bottoms of the opposite bluffs, Shoshoni lodges glowed faint from warming fires within.

"The camp I seen over there, it's about a mile from the top of that bluff," Rockwell said. "Those bluffs, they drop down maybe two hundred feet. It's damn steep, but horses can make it down if you're careful. Once you bottom out, it ain't but a little way to the river."

"How steep are these bluffs, again?" Connor said.

"Depends. You'll want to go down right here where I show you. If the men are careful and let the horses find their way, they can make a trail straight down. But if them pony soldiers of yours don't take care, and try to push their mounts, they'll go down off them bluffs ass over teakettle."

"Is there no other way to reach the river?"

"Sure. Not too far west of there, the bluffs ain't near so steep. There's a wagon road angles down off there, maybe a mile yonder. That'd be where the Montana Road crosses the river."

"Then what the hell's the point of goin' over the edge and down them bluffs?" McGarry said. "Sounds a damn fool idea to me to do that in the dark when you can take a safer route. Why not?"

Rockwell smiled. "If it's surprise you're a-wantin' you won't find it on the road. That's why we're away out here off the road in the first place. You can bet them Shoshoni will have lookouts.

They'll be watchin' that ford. Them Shoshoni ain't blind, and they'll see you coming from that way long before they'll know you're here if you go the way I say." He stared at McGarry until the major looked away, then turned his attention to Connor. "Like I said, if them troopers is careful and give the horses their heads, it'll be all wheat."

Hitch a ride on a high-flying hawk for a trip over this part of the world, and this is what you will see:

The Bear River meanders along a plain a mile to a mile and a half wide, hemmed in by high bluffs. The general direction of its flow here is southwest, but it takes a bend and runs directly west for about a half mile before veering southward for a time, then runs due west for another mile before finally deciding south is the way to go.

Near the end of the first of those westward kinks is a place to cross the river. Not an ideal crossing, but a possible one.

Downstream from the makeshift ford—a mile as the river flows, half that as the hawk flies—Beaver Creek joins Bear River in a marshy mess of cattails and reeds and willows. To reach the join, Beaver Creek flows southeast from out between the bluffs on the other side of the river plain, out of the west, then turns south and runs for three quarters of a mile to meet the river. Along the way, over the eons, Beaver Creek has meandered, cutting a wide ravine several feet deep near the bluffs, becoming shallower as the watercourse approaches Bear River. A mile or so south and west of the ravine, between a ridge rising to the west and the bottomland, is a hot spring.

Between Beaver Creek and the meanders of the river to the northeast is a half-mile wide mostly level plain, with a slight rise from river to creek. Some would see it as an open field across which to mount a charge. Others would view it as a shooting gallery.

"What will we find at the bottom?" Connor said.

"Like I said, we can get across the river there, and Shoshoni camp is maybe a half a mile away. That river'll be froze over partway, and the horses ain't going to like it. They won't want to go in, but there ain't nothing to be done about that. It's the only decent place to cross.

"From there, the Shoshoni horses is beyond the camp, out in the middle of the bottoms," Rockwell said. "Come daylight, you'll see a steamy place where there's warm springs. That's about where the horses ought to be. The camp, most of it, strings out in a ravine along a creek coming out of bluffs on the other side. Ain't much of a creek. I'm told you can step across it, most places. But it, and the camp, is down in a little ravine, and it's good cover.

"The boys tell me there's a mess of willows along that creek and the banks of the ravine, and them Shoshonis will likely be hid up in them if they see you coming, which they will if it's light enough. If they are, it'll be a damn sight easier for them to get a shot at you and your soldiers than for you to see who's doing the shooting, as it ain't likely they'll show themselves."

"How many Indians?" Connor said.

"A bunch of 'em pulled out a few days ago. There's maybe seventy-five, eighty lodges down there now, I'm told. That many lodges, figure four or five hundred Indians. Counting old men and boys big enough to do battle, they'll likely muster two hundred fighters at most."

"I say we form a line parallel to the ravine and march right through the savage bastards," McGarry said. "We'll break them with the first rush, and then it will be a simple matter of mopping up."

"Maybe not so simple as you think," said Rockwell. "I'm guessing they can lay down pretty heavy fire from their hiding places. I don't know as I would want to try them head on."

"But remember, Colonel, that these are savages we face," McGarry said, dismissing the scout by directing his comment to Connor. "They know less of military strategy and tactics than even Rockwell here. In the face of an organized charge, the cowards will turn and run before we even fire a shot, just as they did at Empey's Ferry."

But Rockwell would not be dismissed. "Bear Hunter ain't no fool, and he knows a thing or two about fighting."

"Bullshit, Rockwell. The Indian does not live who can outfight trained troops. I say let's have at them, Colonel Connor."

Connor mulled it over as he tried to better imagine what lay before them. Finally, he said, "My greatest fear, gentlemen, is that the Shoshoni will skedaddle. Major McGarry, at the very least I expect your cavalry troops to pin them down and hold them until the infantry arrives to assist.

"I will stay here with the infantry and wagons and assist Captain Hoyt in getting these wagons moving. We will want those cannons. It sounds as if we could mount a deadly fire from atop the bluffs Rockwell describes. Major, you will lead the cavalry troops. Follow Mister Rockwell's advice as to descending the bluffs and fording the river. Then, deploy skirmishers with an eye to encircling the camp with sufficient force to prevent the Indians from breaking out. At all costs, Major McGarry, you are not to allow the savages to escape this place. Am I clear?"

The major nodded, then reined his horse around and started up the back trail toward the mounted troops. The colonel heeled his horse into motion, but Rockwell stopped him.

"Colonel Connor . . ."

"What is it, Rockwell?"

"Your man McGarry is taking Bear Hunter too lightly. He takes those Indians on head-on, he'll be like a man with a wildcat by the tail wondering how to turn it loose."

"I must place my trust in the major. He has my every confidence. And remember, Rockwell, he is no stranger to the Shoshoni and has licked them before."

"Maybe so. Only this time, Colonel, them Shoshoni down there ain't tied up."

CHAPTER TWENTY-FIVE

The mountain howitzers never made it to the battlefield. Nor did the supply wagons. While gunshots punctuated the morning hours of 29 January 1863, the two cannon were left alone and useless, stuck in the snow six miles away.

Maybe it was the left wheel mired deep in the snow while the right rode high. Or perhaps the opposite. More often it would have been both wheels buried beyond the axles, which attempted to push, pile, plow snow with every attempt at forward motion.

Not that the soldiers did not try to get the guns and wagons through. Artillerymen, teamsters, infantrymen, and horse teams attacked the task with shovels, ropes, pry bars, poles, wagon tongues, extra teams, hands, shoulders, backs, and, even in temperatures below zero, copious quantities of sweat.

Officers, from Colonel Connor down through the ranks, pushed and prodded the soldiers. The air thereabouts sizzled with oaths and profanity, grunts and groans, gees and haws, whip cracks and palm smacks, and, mostly, more cussing and cursing.

But there can be no victory when nature is the enemy, and the enemy is determined. And so, despite best efforts, the mountain howitzers of the California Volunteers saw no action that day.

The cold lay heavy on the lowland when Sagwitch left the

warmth of his lodge in the early hours of morning to answer the call of nature, as all men of his age were wont to do. There was as yet no ribbon of light in the southeastern sky to signal the arrival of dawn, but the chief felt it would not be long in coming.

What the coming day would bring he did not know. On a philosophical level that was true of every day, Sagwitch knew. But not every day dawned with American soldiers no more than ten miles away, and that fact heightened his anxiety.

Most of the village was fast asleep at this hour. A few men and women were still at work with the bullet molds, and some women, habitual early risers like Sagwitch, were stirring around and starting the day's food preparation. After satisfying himself with the well-being of the camp—tentative though it might be— Sagwitch tended to his morning toilet, then climbed out of Beaver Creek ravine and walked away from the village to spend a few minutes alone in the quiet.

Sagwitch crouched on the cold ground and let his eyes adjust to the dim glow of the snow. He scanned the sky for a hint of light. He let his gaze wander along the course of the *Boa Ogoi*, as if the river might carry relief for the anxiety that enveloped him. He inspected the bluffs beyond. Oddly enough, he detected motion there.

A mist rose from the hillside—a thin, almost invisible haze of smoke, or steam, it seemed. He cupped his hands around his eyes to concentrate whatever light might illuminate the misty bluff and mask the light from every other direction. His pupils enlarged slightly as a result, infinitesimally sharpening his vision. But the slight improvement was enough to allow Sagwitch to make sense of what he saw.

What appeared to be smoke was actually an airborne mist of fallen snow, churned back into the air by the hooves of dozens and dozens of horses sliding, skipping, lunging, leaping, bobbing, bouncing down the steep face of the bluffs.

Sagwitch leapt up and ran back to the ravine and through the camp to Bear Hunter's lodge. There was no time to tarry. He burst in unannounced and uninvited in a breach of politeness and protocol and shook the war chief awake.

Within minutes the soldiers—more soldiers than Sagwitch could ever have imagined—would be across the *Boa Ogoi* with only an empty snowfield less than half a mile wide separating them from the Shoshoni camp.

He still hoped that perhaps, maybe, possibly, the troops only wanted to take a few prisoners to satisfy the settlers' complaints. But the knot in the pit of his stomach told him this could be the realization of the vision of Tin Dup.

And the old seer, long gone with the people of Pocatello, was not even here to see his dream come true.

Private Thaddeus Barcafer's heels pummeled his mount's belly. He held the reins outstretched before him and pursed his lips and made kissing sounds at the reluctant horse, which stood trembling at the river's edge, hind legs in a squat and forelegs planted stiff.

"C'mon, you bunch of shirkers, get them across there!" Major McGarry shouted.

The horses already had their blood up from the trip over the edge of the bluffs. Some had carefully picked their way down, cutting back and forth across the steep face. Others had simply hunkered down on their hocks and slid straight down.

Now, having covered maybe fifteen miles through the cold and snow and dark, only to be pushed over the edge of the bluff to make their way down, the cavalry mounts were in no mood for the further discourtesy of a plunge in the icy river.

McGarry rode behind Barcafer and proceeded to whip the soldier's horse across the rump with his bridle reins. "C'mon, you cowardly beast! In you go!"

Instead, the horse reared up, and Barcafer sawed on the reins in a feeble attempt at control that only served to unbalance the bay gelding and force him over backwards. Luckily, the horse missed landing on the soldier in the fall and soon rolled over and found his feet. But Private Barcafer, the wind forced from his lungs, lay in frozen mud on the riverbank trying to recover the ability to breathe.

Another trooper grabbed the loose horse's reins and brought him under control as McGarry turned his attention and the lash of his reins toward Barcafer.

"Get up! Get your sorry ass back in the saddle, and get across the river," he screamed as the soldier shielded his face from the snaking reins, then scrambled to his feet and out of range. "C'mon, dammit, all of you! We can't get anything done on this side of this damn river. The Indians are on the other side, and that is where you damn well better find yourselves! And fast!"

Meanwhile, a few of the mounts had been pushed, pulled, poked, and prodded into the stream. The Bear River was fifty yards wide at the ford. It was frozen over at the edges with ice maybe four inches thick at the verge and growing ever thinner until it disappeared altogether some fifteen or twenty feet out into the current, the result being that the first horses urged onto the ice were doomed to break through, causing further fear and panic.

Once the ice was broken up, the chunks floated away downstream in the steady current, joining the ice and thick slush already in the flow. At its deepest point, the river at this place was between three and four feet deep—not enough depth to cause the crossing horses to lose footing and swim, but deep enough to assure that almost every trooper entering the river would exit with wet feet, bound in river-soaked leather boots that would soon stiffen and freeze in the chill air.

Some were destined for worse. In the cold and dark, as the

horses thrashed in the water, twisting and turning and bumping and dodging, it was perhaps inevitable that riders would be unhorsed to plunge into the freezing stream. And they did. But none was lost. Despite the terror and confusion and the screaming of McGarry and other officers, and the frightened screaming horses, every fallen man was fished out of the stream to be reunited with his horse on the other side of the bitter crossing.

Getting out of the river was no easier than getting in. The opposite side, too, was frozen over a good way out from the bank. Horses reluctantly tested the ice with quivering forelegs only to have it give way, plunging delicate limbs through jagged breaks and back into freezing water. Despite the difficulty, the crossing was eventually accomplished, finally putting the troops within striking distance of their enemy.

Through it all, Porter Rockwell sat his horse calmly and pondered how men who made their living horseback could be so inept at handling the animals.

McGarry steamed and stewed, aware that the ruction created by the crossing had no doubt awakened the Shoshoni camp, alerting his prey to the presence of a predator. As the sky slowly showed the hope of light, he studied the terrain, searching and seeking a way to carry out Connor's orders to trap the savages in their lair, shutting off all avenues of escape.

CHAPTER TWENTY-SIX

Toward, but not at, the end of the long winter night, Connor, in his frustration, watched the sky for the arrival of the dawn. He questioned his decision to leave it to Major McGarry to initiate the action and keep the Shoshoni bottled up until he could reinforce the cavalry troopers with the infantry.

McGarry's four companies of cavalry, diminished by the loss of the frostbitten troopers left behind at Brigham City, mounted only about one hundred and fifty effectives. The added firepower of the infantry would be essential in subduing the savages, and the traffic jam in the snow threatened the very success of the expedition.

The intention had been for the infantry and cavalry columns to arrive at the river simultaneously. Connor's marching orders were that Captain Sam Hoyt and the infantry leave Franklin at one o'clock in the morning with the howitzers and wagons, with the cavalry to follow at four o'clock.

But, at the last minute, Hoyt feared losing the way in the dark and wanted a guide to accompany the column. Connor and Porter Rockwell were well south of town at the bivouac and unaware of the delay until a messenger dispatched by Hoyt arrived with the captain's request. An angry Connor sent Rockwell back to Franklin to recruit a guide from among the settlers.

The scout pounded on the door of the small house occupied by Ed and Joe Nelson. A rarity in Mormon country, the Nelson brothers were bachelors. Each had been married, once. Ed, in

151

fact, had fathered two children. But both men's families had taken sick and died while crossing the plains to Zion and lay in unmarked graves on the high plains. Neither Ed nor Joe had seen fit to take another wife, let alone more than one, and this diminished their standing somewhat in the church. But they were accomplished farmers and handy in other ways, and the men of Franklin had determined the Nelsons were no danger to their wives and daughters, so the men were accepted in the town, where they kept mostly to themselves in the small cabin they shared.

Rockwell pounded the door again but did not wait for an answer, instead barging into the cabin uninvited.

"Ed!" he called. "Joe? Hello!"

He heard grumbling as one of the brothers stumbled into the main room from a lean-to at the opposite end of the house where, apparently, the brothers' sleeping quarters were located. While Rockwell waited, one or the other of the Nelsons scratched a lucifer across the stone of the fireplace and lit a lantern that sat on the mantelshelf.

"Rockwell!" said Ed—at least Rockwell thought it was Ed—squinting through the lantern light. "What the hell are you doing here? My God, man, it's the middle of the night."

"Them infantry soldiers was supposed to be out of here and on the way to the Indian camp more than an hour ago, and they ain't gone yet. The captain all of a sudden decided he wasn't sure of the trail and needed someone to show the way."

By now, Joe—at least Rockwell thought it was Joe—had staggered in from the lean-to, pulling up his trousers with one hand and ruffling his disheveled blond hair with the other.

"So what's that got to do with us?"

"You're going. Either one or both of you."

"The hell you say!" Joe said. "In case you didn't notice, I'm asleep."

152

"Don't get used to it, because it's time to wake up. Get dressed."

"Not a chance, Rockwell. We go nowhere. It's late," Ed said.

"And in case you didn't notice, it's cold," Joe said as he stuck his hands into his armpits.

"I noticed, all right, so you better dress warm. But you better get to it, or you'll be going in your drawers."

"Rockwell, we already did what you asked. Now leave us out of this. We ain't taking no more orders from you—not on the say-so of Bishop Thomas, Peter Maughan, or Brigham Young himself. Now, get out of here. We're going back to bed," Ed said and moved toward the lantern.

"Just hold on there for a minute, both of you," Rockwell said as he pulled a Navy Colt pistol with a sawed-off barrel from his coat pocket and thumbed back the hammer. "I don't know if you Cache Valley boys know much about me, but I been told that I have somewhat of a reputation for persuading folks to do the right thing."

"What you've got, Rockwell, is a reputation as a cold-blooded killer."

"Say it however you want, Joe. The fact is, you or Ed or the both of you is getting dressed right now and showing Captain Hoyt and his soldiers where them Shoshonis is camped. And you had best hurry—unless you care to test this reputation of mine."

So it was that Captain Hoyt and the infantry and the howitzers and the baggage wagons and Ed and Joe Nelson had left Franklin two hours late on the march to Bear River. And on the way they were further delayed by deep cold and deep snow and wheels stuck in snowbanks, pressing their hardest toward the encampment, only to be stymied in the quest, overtaken short of their goal by Major McGarry's cavalry companies and the wrath of Colonel Patrick Connor.

Frustration overflowing, the colonel finally lost all hope of freeing the wagons in time. Forsaking the work in favor of fighting, he ordered the soldiers to battle. As the winter sky in the southeast showed the first hint of light, the infantry troops double-timed through the snow while Connor, from horseback, drove them on with continuous tongue lashing.

Six miles away, the cavalry milled in fear and confusion in the icy waters of Bear River, a mere half mile from the Shoshoni camp.

By the time the crossing was complete, the presence of the troops was, of course, no secret and the element of surprise no longer among McGarry's weapons, if ever it had been. But he expected the resistance of the Indians would be short-lived if not insignificant.

The troops milled about, stomping feet and flapping arms in vain attempts to ward off the cold. As sub-zero temperatures turned water to ice, painfully cold and wet boots and trousers became stiff and encrusted with ice. Virtually every trooper's feet were wet, and a few who had been thrown from their horses in the crossing were soaked head to toe.

Splash and spray had showered man and horse alike, so beads of ice clung to clothing, hair, leather, and fabric. The cold and the wet and the discomfort slowed the assembly of the reluctant troops, and McGarry's ire managed to hurry them along only a little. But, with the enemy at hand, the major was ready to pitch in and so abused and harangued the men toward readiness, ordering them to check their loads and ready their weapons.

The sky continued to lighten slowly but surely as his officers regrouped the men and formed into their companies. Every fourth man was detailed to hold the horses, the other three to join the offensive against the village.

McGarry's study of the terrain continued, hoping the

landscape would suggest where troops should be deployed to pin down the Indians. Although not visible because of its concealment in the shallow ravine, the glow of campfires made the location of the Shoshoni camp clear, spread as it was along Beaver Creek for nearly half a mile. Just about the time the troops were organized to the major's satisfaction and a plan was coming together in his mind, a murmur bubbled up among the soldiers and rippled through the assembled troops.

McGarry wheeled his horse in the direction of the Indian camp to find the cause.

Bear Hunter and Sagwitch scurried through the village, calling the men to arms and telling the women and children to find shelter in the lodges and any other place that offered security. The fighting men gathered what few functioning rifles they owned, most of those of a kind now so obsolete that settlers were willing to give them in trade to the Indians. Other firearms of more recent vintage had been plundered during raids on settlements and wagon trains. Most of the fighters, however, carried only bows and arrows—lethal enough within range, and quicker to reload and fire than the rifles—and hatchets and clubs and lances for fighting in close quarters.

Bear Hunter deployed those with the most effective firearms along the edge of the ravine. The men looped and tied willow branches to create rests to steady their rifles and laid by powder and balls for reloading. Dispersed among them were fighters with their bows.

Among the younger men were some who argued with Bear Hunter's strategy. They urged offense, rather than defense.

"Look at them!" one said. "Those soldiers over there are in disarray! If we attack, we can kill them all!"

"Can you not see their numbers?" Bear Hunter said. "They are more than we are, and they have better weapons. Our attack would be repelled, and with much loss of life. It is too risky."

"Bear Hunter, you have become like an old woman!"

The old leader only stared at the impolite boy, a young man who had raided with others of his kind but knew nothing of real fighting.

Most of the men chose to follow Bear Hunter's advice, but, still, there was much discussion. Sagwitch urged caution, still believing, or hoping, that the soldiers would talk before fighting. He lobbied for restraint, encouraging all the fighting men to follow Bear Hunter, and to fight the Americans only if attacked.

But, as the hustle and bustle of the preparations carried on, a young man rode through the village, painted for war, the buttstock of his rifle standing on his thigh, bow strung and looped over his shoulder, quivered arrows hanging from the other shoulder, Green River knife sheathed at his waist.

His horse splashed across Beaver Creek, and the rider reined up at the edge of the lodges, near where the men readied for whatever was to come.

Rifle raised high, he shouted, "You cowards can hide in camp like women if you so choose. As for me, I will challenge the *Toquashes*!"

McGarry, alerted by the mumbling among the men, looked toward the Shoshoni encampment to find the source of the commotion.

There, prancing along the edge of Beaver Creek ravine, was a war horse, carrying a Shoshoni warrior decked out in full battle regalia. As the warrior promenaded before the assembled troops, he waved a rifle high overhead. Dangling from the barrel was what looked to be a scalp with long, blond hair, erstwhile property of some unfortunate white woman.

McGarry's slow burn burst into flame, his consideration of strategy and tactics withering in fire and ire. The Shoshoni started shouting in respectable English, taunting the troops with insults and obscene jests and catcalls. Other voices, obscured in the willows lining the ravine, joined his. Then the mounted warrior reined up and launched into a chant—a mockery of the dress parades and drill of which Colonel Connor was so fond:

"Fours left! Fours right! Come on, you California sonsabitches, fight!"

CHAPTER TWENTY-SEVEN

Casting aside any further thoughts of tactics or strategy, McGarry, now at a rolling boil, ordered the soldiers into skirmish lines. Even before the troopers finished assembling, he turned to the bugler next to him and said through clenched teeth, "Private Hupfner, sound the charge."

The open lines started slowly as icy feet found their rhythm—stiff, frosty leather tramping across the snowfield, bayonets fixed and rifles ready. The lines moved faster as tired, sore, chilled muscles loosened up. McGarry, on horseback, urged them on.

Along the fringe of Beaver Creek ravine, the Shoshoni fighters waited, concealed by the line of willows. They felt the earth tremble as the tramping feet carrying their waves of steel drew ever nearer. Muscles tightened and jaws clenched as the drumming built under the feet and under the knees and under the elbows and under the bellies of the men who stood and squatted and kneeled and lay among the willows watching the drum, drum, drumming lines of soldiers move up the slight rise out of the misty dawn.

The deadly line pounded, pounded across the snowy field toward the other line—the line of willows that marked the edge of Beaver Creek ravine where the lodges stood and the women and children waited, feeling but unable to see the pounding approach of the troopers. And the line of Shoshoni men in the willows watched and waited.

Watched steam rise from tunics warmed by body heat and

stream from flared nostrils and twist and spin and wisp away into the winter air.

Watched tiny beads of river ice break from cloth and leather and hair and beards to float and glow like sparkly trade goods tossed wholesale by the soldiers.

Watched gunmetal glint in grasping hands, gripped fists wrapped around wood and steel, bayonet tips shining as the lines approached ever faster.

And the Shoshoni men watched and waited.

Waited as the drumming line pounded closer and the troopers grew faces.

Waited as tired eyes, wide with fear or excitement or lust, grew wider and white like the snow through which the men moved.

Waited until scalps and side whiskers and mustaches turned all the shades of brown and blond and red in the dim light.

And the Shoshoni men waited and watched some more.

Sitting in his saddle among the horse holders and held horses, Rockwell could see what was bound to happen. The cavalry troopers drew ever nearer the willows along Beaver Creek. The Indians did nothing. Soon, he knew, all hell would break loose.

He had to admire Bear Hunter's ploy. Somehow, the old chief must have sensed Major McGarry's temper and added it to his weapons. And, now that it had been effectively employed, the next weapon in his arsenal would be deployed in a matter of seconds.

But those seconds stretched interminably. The lines of soldiers moved ever closer to the line of willows, so close that, for an instant, Rockwell thought he had misread the Shoshoni intentions and that maybe McGarry was right, and the troopers would march through the encampment untouched.

Then he saw the willows belch countless puffs of smoke.

Troopers up and down the line fell. He watched soldiers tip sideways, fall forward, and pitch over backward. He saw soldiers fall to their knees, rise again, and fall, nevermore to rise.

Then, sound rolled across the snowfield and engulfed Rockwell where he sat his horse on the bank of the Bear River. First to arrive was what sounded like the roar of a dozen cannon, but it was rifle fire—the sound of rifles spitting lead in near perfect unison. Hard on the heels of the first salvo came the *pop-pop-pop* of rapid and continuing fire from the willows.

McGarry's anger turned to horror as soldiers fell all around him. "Bugler!" he called. "Bugler!"

No response.

And he saw why. Adolph Hupfner was kneeling in the snow some ten yards to his rear, left hand grasping the mangled remains of his right arm. Stunned and shocked, the private looked around helplessly for the bugle, unable to find its hiding place in the snow.

The major raced up and down the length of the ragged lines, calling out to the men to regroup at the river crossing, and dispatching every aide and officer he could locate to spread the word further.

The pristine field that minutes ago had separated the cavalry from the Shoshoni was now littered with wounded, dying, and dead soldiers. Scarlet splotches spoiled the white of the snow.

Shattered soldiers struggled to rise, heads and bodies slamming repeatedly to the ground in failure and frustration. Legs milled, hands grasped to find something, anything to cling to. Others limped and hobbled across the field, carrying themselves on torn and broken legs. Still others ran blindly, guided only by panic. McGarry watched most of the men moving toward the river while a few others, disoriented, were running nowhere but away. He saw Porter Rockwell riding along the riverbank with the bridle reins of two runaway horses in hand, two of several mounts that escaped and bolted from the horse holders in the confusion.

And the bullets from the willows continued to fly. The soldiers had no targets at which to return fire; some shot blindly into the willows with the belief that so many Shoshoni lurked there that any bullet fired in that direction would have to hit someone.

Behind the willows, the Shoshoni were jubilant. Bear Hunter's plan had worked to perfection. Unexpected, but fortuitous, the horseback teasing and taunting of the young man had enraged the leader of the soldiers.

And, like all Americans, he had underestimated the strength and fighting skill of the Indians.

Bear Hunter walked the length of the ravine, out of sight of the soldiers and safe from their bullets. He encouraged the fighting men in the willows to keep firing but to choose their targets carefully to conserve ammunition, which had been in short supply even before the fight had started. Too, he encouraged the women among the lodges, who continued to melt down scarce supplies of lead and mold bullets as they had done through much of the night.

Near the southern end of the camp, closest to the *Boa Ogoi*, he saw Sagwitch step out of the willows and onto the brushy floor of the ravine.

"It is as you said, Bear Hunter," Sagwitch said. "The soldiers came to kill us all."

"Yes. I did not think they would come this far in the cold for any other reason."

"Did you know that their leader is the one who tied up and shot those four and dumped the bodies in the river?"

"He is also the one who does not respect a truce," Bear Hunter said. "Remember when I told you how that soldier seized me and One-Eyed Tom and Ray Diamond from under a white flag and held us hostage overnight to trade us for that half-white son of Washakie's sister? He was that one."

"I have always thought you were lucky to get out of that one alive."

"Yes. I think this soldier enjoys killing."

"Well, he is getting plenty of killing today—but not the kind he expected."

"I hope he has had enough, Sagwitch. Otherwise, it may be our people who are killed. We have used up much of our ammunition already."

"They will not come back. These white men have no stomach for death when it is their own who are dying."

The sound of rifle fire turned to silence as the troopers regrouped at the river, no longer within sure-shot range of the Shoshoni weapons. McGarry rode among the men, seeking out his officers. Captain McLean was shot and lying wounded on the field. Two lieutenants were missing. At least a dozen troopers were reported killed, twice that many wounded. Some of the injured had made it back on their own, some with the help of their comrades. Others lay in the snow of the battlefield, beyond reach or assistance. Their cries would occasionally prompt a soldier or a group of solders to venture out on a rescue effort, but a few well-placed shots from out of the willows would soon enough send them scrambling back.

McGarry sent some of the troopers with slight wounds to take over for the horse holders and ordered the officers to form the men into skirmish lines and advance again on the willows.

"You don't want to do that, Major."

McGarry turned stiffly toward the high-pitched voice. Rockwell sat casually in the saddle, the reins of the two runaway horses still in hand.

"And just why the hell not?"

"You never had enough men to take them head-on in the first place. Now you ain't even got as many as you started with."

"Rockwell, you've proved your value this morning as a horse holder. I suggest you stick to that and leave the fighting to the army."

"You go after them Indians like you're planning, and you'll wish to hell you had me and all these other horse holders on the business end of a carbine. But it still wouldn't be enough. Sooner or later, you're going to have get around the sides to flush them out of that ravine. You might as well get it done before anybody else gets killed for no good reason."

"You think so, do you. Well I'll tell you what, you Mormon sonofabitch, you just sit there on your horse and watch."

So, he did. Rockwell watched the line of skirmishers move forward in fits and starts, the men running ahead in a squat, dropping to the snow, then getting up again and going on. And, as he expected, as soon as the troopers got close enough to the Shoshoni riflemen, hidden behind the edge of the ravine and screened by the willows, the Indians started firing, and the soldiers started falling.

Mounted officers dashed back and forth along the line, dodging bullets and urging the men on, probing the Shoshoni defenses here, then there, pushing forward only to be pushed back.

The Shoshoni held. The cavalry troopers could not know if even one of their bullets had found a target—but they knew all too well that all too many Shoshoni bullets had. While this advance was not as deadly for the troopers as the first—the soldiers, if not McGarry, having learned a lesson—there were still too many men with shattered bones and furrowed flesh and bloody, gaping holes that should not be there.

Eventually, Major McGarry recognized the futility of his strategy. He issued orders to move as many of the dead and wounded off the field as possible while the rest of the troopers held their positions and poured enough fire toward the Shoshoni camp to discourage any Indians who might consider leaving.

No one in the ravine, however, was contemplating any such move.

"They are falling back again!" Lehi said.

"I hope they have had enough. Maybe this time they will stay back and leave us alone."

"But this is a great victory, Bear Hunter. The more the soldiers attack, the more of them we can kill."

"We can only kill as many as we have bullets. Already some of the men are shooting arrows. We will not be able to hold them off much longer. If they are determined, it will be a bad thing for us."

Just then Sagwitch came running up the ravine. "Bear Hunter! Lehi!" was all he managed to get out before stopping to catch his breath. "*Toquashes!*" he finally managed to gasp, pointing northeastward toward the bluffs. "Soldiers!"

Bear Hunter's heart sank as he saw dozens of infantrymen making their way down the steep hill toward the river. He knew it would only be a matter of time before they were across the *Boa Ogoi* and ready to fight. And he knew there were not enough bullets left in the camp to kill them all.

Colonel Connor quickly took matters in hand at the river ford, ordering the horse holders across the stream with the cavalry mounts to ferry the infantry troops to the battlefield. Now, in daylight, with benefit of experience, and resigned to the task, the horses offered little resistance, and the soldiers soon accomplished the crossing, bolstering the fighting force with more than three score of fresh troops—as fresh, that is, as men can be after five hours of wrestling wheeled vehicles and marching and double timing through feet of snow in sub-zero temperatures before sunrise.

Those cavalry officers still ambulatory and the newly arrived infantry officers huddled with the colonel as soon as he could gather them. He requested an estimate of the casualties and the nature of the fight up till then. He sought opinions on the characteristics of the Shoshoni position and studied the terrain. Never one to foster debate or await consensus in military matters, Connor decided a course of action within minutes and proceeded to issue orders.

"Major McGarry, you are to select twenty of the best cavalry fighters we've got. Mount up and ride to the north, climb the bluffs until you are beyond the Indian encampment, then cut west to the creek. Double back to the south, then dismount and work your way on foot down the ravine until you are able to pour enfilading fire into the Shoshoni stronghold.

"At the same time, you, Lieutenant Clark, are to take a detail and deploy them across the creek where it joins the river, bottling up the Shoshoni at the south end. Lieutenant Quinn, gather your men and follow Clark, but take your troops well beyond the creek and move north toward the camp, cutting off any escape to the west. The rest of you are to distribute your troops along the existing front. Captain Hoyt, take the right flank and be ready to push in and join McGarry as soon as possible.

"Gentlemen, once all are in position, the Indians will be covered from every direction with nowhere to go. You will attack in unison when Major McGarry commences firing. We will take no prisoners, accept no surrender, give no quarter. No further orders will be needed, and none will be issued. Am I clear?"

Sporadic fire continued along the front as the soldiers deployed according to the colonel's orders. The Shoshoni chiefs watched the movement of the troops. "They have been quiet too long. The soldiers are not attacking. I am afraid they are up to something," Sagwitch said.

"Look! They are splitting up," Lehi said. "We can attack each group in turn and wipe them out one by one."

Bear Hunter did not share Lehi's excitement. He understood at once what the soldiers were planning, and his mind raced for a means to counter their strategy. He saw that they would be cut off from the horse herd, which milled nervously south and west of the camp near the hot springs. As was always the case in Bear Hunter's camp, there were dozens of horses staked out among the lodges for easy access. But there were not enough for all the people, and soon there would be no way out anyway. The old chief could not think how to respond.

"Can you not see what they are doing, Lehi?" he said.

"Yes, I see! They are spreading themselves too thin. They did not have enough soldiers to break through before, and now they are divided. As I said, we can attack in force and overwhelm them, one group at a time. Or we can stay where we are and kill them when they come to us. Even without the protection of the willows, if we stay in the ravine we should be able to hold them off."

What Lehi said sounded good. But Bear Hunter did not believe it. "What you say may be true. I do not think we should attack, or we will leave the women and children unprotected. And maybe we can hold the soldiers off as long as the bullets last.

"But I think the soldiers will attack as one and draw ever closer, and we will be caught like buffalo in a surround. Maybe they will push us out of the camp and kill us out in the open. Maybe they will come into the camp and kill us here."

"You have given up! We must not give up!" Sagwitch said. "I did not think this fight would come. But now that it is here, I will never stop fighting. Never. If I did not know you so well, Bear Hunter I would think you have become a coward. We cannot surrender to the *Toquashes*."

Surrender, thought Bear Hunter. Sagwitch thinks I want to surrender. What I think is that it would not do any good to surrender—it would not save a single life.

But he would not say so. Instead, he stepped close to the younger chief, then leaned even closer into his face and, through clenched teeth, said, "Do not even pretend to insult me, Sagwitch. I said nothing about giving up. I am not afraid to die. And the soldiers will pay dearly if they are to take my life. But we must figure out what we can do to protect the old people and the babies and the women from the soldiers. Because the soldiers will be coming."

Within minutes, the chiefs had dispatched runners up and down the half-mile length of the camp. The fighting men were to be distributed around the perimeter, with the noncombatants clustering in the center. The warriors would fight off the army as long as possible, then fall back and establish a new defensive line. The Shoshoni had stopped the soldiers so far, had, in fact, given the army the worst of it. Maybe, if their ammunition would not hold out, their luck would.

CHAPTER TWENTY-EIGHT

From his position in the shallow defile between the bluffs that became Beaver Creek ravine, Major McGarry could not see if the other officers had yet deployed their troops as ordered. Nor could he see the defensive preparations underway in the Shoshoni camp.

He did not care, in either case.

He had had enough of watching California Volunteers die at the hands of these savages, and he was not going to wait any longer than necessary to avenge his fallen comrades. As soon as the men dismounted and tied their mounts, they spread out and started down the ravine, rifles at the ready and pistols close at hand.

The soldiers quickly worked their way from cover to cover, dodging in and out of the cedar trees and thick brush up the side hills and the willows along the creek bottom. No lodges were in sight as yet; still, they expected some resistance from pickets. None came. They were almost upon the first lodge before drawing fire, but it was intense when it came. The burst of fire, though, was brief, and McGarry pushed his men onward, exacting a heavy toll on the retreating warriors.

The attackers made their way a few yards farther down the ravine, and McGarry could see Captain Hoyt's infantry troops rushing in from his left. And the Shoshoni continued to retreat, stopping only occasionally to return fire. Arrows were coming now as often as bullets, and McGarry sensed the Indians' ammunition was nearly spent; the realization prompted him to push the men harder and faster into the camp.

When the fire commenced pouring out from between the bluffs, Quinn and his detail pressed in from the west. And, from the east, infantry troops under the command of Captain George Price charged across the open field between the ravine and the river. Again, they encountered heavy fire from the willows. But while the resistance was severe it was short-lived, and the soldiers pushed through into the ravine leaving dozens of dead Shoshoni in their path.

For more than two hours the Shoshoni had whipped the soldiers. Now, with army bullets ripping through the air thick as hailstones from all directions, and the Shoshoni lacking the ability to match the volume of fire laid down by the California Volunteers, the tide of the battle turned.

And it turned into a massacre.

Bear Hunter watched helplessly as his fighters tried to withstand the onslaught of soldiers. Already, Lehi was dead from six bullets in his head, chest, and belly. He did not know where Sagwitch was fighting or if he, too, was lost. Never in all his years as war chief and leader of all the bands of Shoshoni in the Bear River country had he ever felt so helpless.

Sagwitch knelt in the brush at the lower end of the camp, firing arrows into the approaching soldiers as quickly as he could, pausing only long enough to make sure of each shot. A young man leading a horse stopped beside him. "Sagwitch!" he said, panting for breath. "You must take this horse and make your escape!"

The leader brushed aside the proffered reins. "No! I must fight. We all must fight. These *Toquashes* mean to kill us all! We must fight to protect the women and children."

"We will fight, Sagwitch. But Lehi is dead. I do not know

where Bear Hunter is. Someone must survive to lead The People."

Sagwitch shook his head. "There will be no people to lead if we do not fight."

The young man insisted, and one of the women took his side, telling Sagwitch that some of The People had made it to the river and were escaping, or hiding in rushes in the river.

Sagwitch relented. With bow in hand, he swung onto the horse's back like a much younger man and rode toward the river as his people, darting about through the brush to escape the flying bullets, urged him on.

Balls from the *Toquash* guns whistled and hissed all about him. He heard the thwack of lead hitting horseflesh as the horse staggered. The reins fell from his grip as a bullet shattered his hand. His mount's forelegs buckled. His knees hit the ground, and Sagwitch stepped off as the dying horse rolled to its side.

A woman leading another horse ran to him, holding the frightened, flighty horse as Sagwitch mounted. He managed to turn the horse toward the river but had little control over the panicked horse, too young to be well trained. The horse darted through the brush, ducking, diving, and leaping over and around every obstacle. Sagwitch struggled to keep his seat, his bloody, broken hand lacking strength to grip rein or mane but desperately grasping both.

The pony's terror-driven dash proved a godsend, somehow escaping the fire of the soldiers' rifles and slipping through their lines. With a fearful leap, the horse flew off the riverbank, landing with an icy splash in the thick of the current. Sagwitch slid off the side to be towed along. From out of the reeds at river's edge, a woman appeared and grabbed a handful of the horse's floating tail. The mount swam a few strokes until finding bottom, then Sagwitch swung his leg over the horse's back, urging the pony with pounding heels through the cold stream, pulling the woman along in its wake as bullets ripped the air around them. As the distance from the fight grew, the soldiers lost interest, and Sagwitch was saved.

Bear Hunter watched the soldiers pushing into the village, forcing his people down the ravine toward the river. But there was no refuge to be found there, and soldiers moving up the ravine from that direction shot the people down in bloody piles.

A young fighter, with no more than sixteen years, tried to climb the steep bank of the ravine in a place where no steps had been cut. As he clawed his way toward the top, bullets turned his back into a sieve, and the man slid slowly back down the clay bank, leaving his lifeblood behind in a gory trail.

The Shoshoni milled all around Bear Hunter in panic and confusion. Warriors fought fiercely with any and every possible weapon. Some still had powder and bullets, and some of these found targets, killing and wounding soldiers. He saw other soldiers with arrow wounds. He saw one of his fighting men bash a trooper with a cooking pot. Lances, clubs, hatchets, rocks, knives, clubbed rifles—all became weapons to fight off the attackers but were no match the soldiers' guns.

As the fighting became tight, even hand to hand, the soldiers discarded their rifles and carbines, finding revolvers a more effective weapon in close quarters. Bear Hunter knocked a trooper to the ground with his empty rifle, which he raised again to brain the man. But, as the chief unleashed a vicious downstroke, the soldier managed to get off a pistol shot that ripped through Bear Hunter's side. His blow landed, but the power of the swing and the force of the bullet combined to take him down, as well.

Even then, the old man was not finished. Not yet. He struggled back to his feet and stumbled around in shock. The sound of screaming, of smashing, of running, of shouting, of shooting seemed strangely muffled and distant. He stumbled along, seemingly unaware of a second bullet ripping through his shoulder. The chief tried to tell his people to run, to try to escape, but he could not tell if they heard him, or even if he had spoken.

He was nearly run over by a warrior on horseback, racing through the camp dodging lodges and people as best he could. That is dangerous, thought Bear Hunter. He should know better than to ride so fast in the camp. Young men are so foolish. The rider found what he was looking for—a young woman, his beloved, Bear Hunter supposed. He grabbed the girl by the arm and lifted her onto the horse behind him and raced off to the southwest. Somehow, they made it out of the camp and through the soldier line. But many of the soldiers turned their rifles on him, and bullets chased the pair toward the river.

Although the horse was by now far away, Bear Hunter still saw it clearly—every rippling muscle, every reaching hoof, every hair in the flying tail. He was surprised to see so well—better than he had in years . . . better, maybe, than he ever had.

He saw the horse hesitate, then break through the ice and splash into the shallow water at the river's edge.

He saw flying particles of ice and droplets of water catch the light and twinkle like stars.

He saw the beautiful fringe on the woman's buckskin dress waving slowly, delicately in the breeze. He saw the tender hollow at the back of her knees as she pressed them against the horse's flank, and the tautness in her arms around the man's waist.

And he saw the bullet dimple her dress, then break through and penetrate the flesh of her back between the shoulder blades. The young man reached around and grasped her dress, tried to keep her aboard the horse, but she was no longer in her body, and it soon splashed into the river and spun slowly away downstream.

★ ★ ★ ★ ★

While the soldiers had the upper hand and the outcome of the fight was determined, it did not all go their way. Lieutenant Quinn, mounted and running down and gunning down escaping Indians on the snowfields west of the camp, had his horse shot from under him. Two of his troopers were shot out of the saddle and seriously wounded. A Captain McGee took a bullet in the groin. A private, shot from point-blank range in the chest, survived because a cartridge case in his pocket deflected the bullet. Price lost eight men of his command killed or wounded in close fighting in the willows.

But the bulk of the dying was accomplished by the Shoshoni. Bear Hunter stumbled over the carcasses of dozens of his people as he staggered around in the camp, shooing children into the lodges, telling some people to lie in the snow and play dead and others to make their way to the river.

He hoped some would make it to the river and escape downstream, even though he could see soldiers standing along the banks shooting at them, laughing as if they were taking target practice. One Shoshoni man had made it, he knew, by swimming away under a buffalo robe that interfered with the bullets. He saw a woman, shot in one arm and carrying a baby in the other, duck under overhanging reeds along the riverbank. He did not know if the cold water would force them out to die under the guns, or freeze them to death in their hiding place.

Another woman and small child waded into the stream. A bullet blasted the infant's head into a bloody pulp. The mother, howling in despair, released the child and watched it float away, trailing a scarlet wake in the dark water. Her next scream was cut short by a bullet piercing her throat. She collapsed in the water, and Bear Hunter watched the blouse of her buckskin dress balloon above the stream flow, the rest of the woman concealed beneath the surface.

Other riflemen laughed and made wagers as they picked off Indians escaping up Cedar Ridge and the steep bluffs west of the camp. Who can hit that one highest up? How far will that one's body roll? Can you kill that one before she reaches that cedar tree? Can you shoot that one clean in the head from this distance?

He saw troopers empty their revolvers into the bodies of panicked Indians—men, women, and children alike—then stop, reload, and do it again. And Bear Hunter felt strangely sad as the soldiers reloaded. Their hands were cold and clumsy in the frigid air, and he saw caps and cartridges drop to the ground and left where they lay. My people could use those bullets and that powder, he thought. Someone should pick those cartridges up before they get trampled and lost.

But not all the ammunition was spilled in the snow. Most made it into a chamber, eventually to take its turn under the hammer, finally to find a place in a Shoshoni body. One such bullet blasted apart Bear Hunter's thigh, and his leg collapsed under him and left him sitting awkwardly in the snow, unable to rise and wondering what he could do now to save some of his people.

CHAPTER TWENTY-NINE

With the situation well in hand, Major McGarry took a pause from shooting Indians and called several of his troopers to gather around. As he carefully pushed fresh cartridges into his revolver, he ordered the men to holster their guns and arrange to move the wounded soldiers off the battlefield and transport them to where the other injured waited near the river ford.

"Aw, Major, we want to keep fighting," one complained.

"The fighting is over, boys. It's down to killing now," McGarry said.

"You're right, sir, and that's what we came for," said one.

"Don't deny us a bit of a frolic, Major," another said.

"All right men, I'll tell you what. Reload your weapons and go kill enough of these vermin to empty them again. Then, by God, you will get these wounded men to where they can get some help, or I'll have your asses. Agreed?"

"Yes, sir!" they said. And they did as they were told. Some of them, anyway. Others took the opportunity to reload again, and maybe again, emptying round after round after round into the heads and chests and backs of Shoshoni cowering in lodges, crouching in the willows, running away, begging for mercy, or whatever else they could think to do in the seconds before they died.

The soldiers no longer sought cover or concealment from which to fire but walked boldly through the camp firing at will. Many of the infantrymen tired of reloading rifle and pistol alike so instead put fixed bayonets on their rifles to bloody use. Dead Indians were so thick on the ground, some in bloody piles, that it was impossible to walk ten yards in any direction without having to change course to avoid treading on a corpse.

And there were Indians lying in the snow only pretending to be dead. Once discovered, these were dispatched with a shot, a thrust. Captain Hoyt encountered one such—a boy, no more than ten years old, lying still as death but with frightened eyes wide open and darting about. The captain took aim, and the boy's eyes slowly closed. He lowered the pistol. After a time— only seconds, probably, but it seemed hours to both—the boy's eyes opened again, and again Hoyt pointed the pistol at a point just between and above those eyes. And, again, the boy's eyes closed, squinted in fear against the expected bullet. But the shot never came. And, when the boy looked again, the captain was walking away.

Most of the troopers rampaging through the Shoshoni encampment had long since lost any sense of discipline. Women were thrust to the ground, their clothing ripped asunder, held down to struggle against the sick pleasure taken by the soldiers. Other women who resisted too vigorously were shot or stabbed or slashed, then raped as their lives slipped away.

Even babies, toddlers, and children were dispatched. Babies became playthings in a loathsome game, tossed back and forth from soldier to soldier to soldier before being killed. Others were grasped by the feet and swung in a deadly arc, brains bashed out against stones.

Bear Hunter sat like a statue where he had fallen. He thought for a time that he must have become invisible, as the soldiers were all around but ignored him. Weak from his wounds and from loss of blood, the old chief was somewhat detached from what happened around him, yet, on another level, his senses remained razor sharp. Finally, he was noticed by a group of three soldiers. One of them reached out with his pistol barrel and prodded the old man's shoulder.

"Hey, you old geezer, you alive?"

"Maybe he's asleep. This will wake him up," one of the soldiers said as he pressed his bayonet into Bear Hunter's chest with enough force to tear through the fabric of his shirt and break the skin underneath.

"Damn!" said another. "Maybe he is dead. Either that, or he's a tough old bird."

The first soldier decided to try his pistol again and see if he could get a rise. This time, though, he swung it in a short, swift arc and laid the barrel upside the Indian's head.

"Would you look at that. He don't even flinch," he said and laid on another blow for good measure. And, again, the bayonet probed his chest and, failing to elicit any response, poked a few holes in the chief's back instead.

Still, the old man sat and wondered what these white men were up to, and why they did not kill him. Some part of him wanted to lash out at them, to inflict pain to repay the pain they gave him, but his body did not seem connected to him anymore, and, besides, he could not feel the pain he knew was there.

While two of the troopers continued hitting him, both with their hands and with the pistol, he watched curiously as the third, the one with the bayonet, propped the weapon into the flames of a fire from a blazing lodge.

He took a blow full in the face and felt blood gush from his nose. The trooper punched him again, and Bear Hunter felt teeth crumble. Still, the pain seemed distant, as if felt by someone else. The torment continued until the soldier at the fire returned. The tip of the bayonet glowed red, the shade deepening as it cooled along its length.

"Hold his head," the trooper said, and the soldier behind the old chief roughly grabbed a hank of his gray-shot hair and twisted, pulling his head back and neck taut. Flesh sizzled and the stink of a branding corral filled the air as the rifleman prodded Bear Hunter's ear. Satisfied the point had found the mark, he leaned into it with his weight and thrust the bayonet into the Shoshoni chief's head so deep that it ripped out through the other ear, blood and brain matter sizzling and smoking and stinking on the hot steel. Bear Hunter still wondered what had happened to him as he tipped over dead in the snow.

Two hours had passed since Major McGarry's troops had burst out of Beaver Creek ravine as it exited the bluffs above the camp. From that moment on, the Shoshoni cause had been lost. Now, four hours since the morning's initial foray, the fury that had driven the soldiers was dying out. Most of the troopers stopped shooting, stopped killing, and turned their attention to saving their wounded comrades and removing the bodies of those killed. But only the soldiers—no thought was given to treating the wounded Shoshoni beyond, perhaps, a death blow. Litters were assembled from overcoats and rifles to carry away the wounded soldiers. Some suffered more from the cold than their wounds, having lain unprotected in the snow for hours.

By the time all the California Volunteers were accounted for, fourteen were dead and some fifty wounded, a few so severely that they, too, would probably die. Another seventy or eighty were in such pain and discomfort from frozen feet they were determined unfit for duty and left with the wounded.

But not all the soldiers gave up the killing. Blood lust still filled some, and they yet ranged through the ravaged campsite like a pack of wolves. Feeling merciful, they put wounded Indians out of their misery, a blow to the head with a sharp ax being the preferred method.

Lodges were destroyed, and the soldiers took satisfaction in the fact that some of the lodge covers they burned were fashioned from wagon canvas stolen, they assumed, from slaughtered emigrants; some were even marked with the names of the former owners. And among the arrows, buffalo robes, knives, hatchets, beads, and gewgaws the troopers plundered from the lodges as trophies, they found mirrors and blankets and combs and cooking utensils that provided further evidence that these Indians had robbed and killed whites.

Ed and Joe Nelson had sat through the morning perched partway up the bluff east of the camp where they had stayed after guiding the infantry, transfixed as they watched the battle unfold. Now they walked through the camp, revolted by what they had witnessed and what they saw there. They determined that at least two hundred and fifty—perhaps as many as three hundred—Shoshoni bodies were strewn about the ground, nearly a hundred of them women and children. And they had watched many others, fifty or more, they thought, float away down the river, dead or dying.

Others arrived at a different body count. A San Francisco newspaper correspondent who was there with the troopers reported two hundred sixty-seven Shoshoni dead and allowed that maybe ten women and a few children had been accidentally killed. Colonel Connor's official report listed two hundred and twenty-four dead on the field. An aide concurred and revised the figure upward by fifty to account for the bodies lost in the river. Their reports did not discriminate by age or sex.

Connor again assembled his officers to issue orders for the remainder of the day. Major McGarry was to direct a salvage operation to the Indian camp and the surrounding countryside to gather horses, food, and other useful goods and prepare them for transport back to Camp Douglas.

"Sir, what about the survivors?" McGarry said.

"Leave them be, unless you encounter men of fighting age. Kill them."

"I meant about the food, sir, and blankets."

"Leave some. Enough for them to survive. But just enough. Destroy the lodges. Detail some men to haul the poles here for firewood. We'll need that and more tonight if we are to keep from freezing."

Connor looked around and spotted Porter Rockwell sitting horseback at the edge of the assembly and summoned him. "Mister Rockwell, we need transportation for the dead and wounded and those with frostbitten feet. We may have more than a hundred infantry and cavalry men who marched or rode here who will be unable to return as they came and so will require transport. We will be needing, I judge, no fewer than ten wagons for the men.

"And there will be the bounty. Accompany Major McGarry for a brief reconnaissance of the camp and estimate the amount of goods to be hauled and add sufficient wagons to your requisition to accomplish it. Commandeer as many wagons outfitted with runners as you deem necessary. And, of course, teams and drivers. They are to accompany us as far south as proves necessary and will be compensated for their trouble. Am I clear?"

"I'll give it a try, Colonel."

"Trying will not accomplish our purpose. It is imperative that you arrive back here as early as possible in the morning with the wagons."

"I doubt folks in town give a shit what's imperative to you and what ain't."

"It is up to you to see that they do."

"Like I said, I'll do what I can. But they weren't in any mood to do you any favors when you got here, and when word gets around what you've done they'll be less likely."

"Whatever do you mean? The settlers wanted the Shoshoni subdued, and by God they are subdued!"

"They never said they wanted women and babies slaughtered,

or girls abused or old men tortured."

"You are a fine one to talk about killing, Rockwell."

Rockwell glared at the colonel with enough intensity to melt ice. "There's killing, and then there's killing."

"You are out of line. I should not have to remind you that the army is not paying you for your impertinence or your opinions."

McGarry flashed the guide a rude grin as the two reined their horses around to attend to their respective errands.

CHAPTER THIRTY

Even as McGarry led the detail of troopers back into the Shoshoni camp to confiscate usable goods, other of the soldiers were still ravaging the site and the survivors.

"C'mon man, get it over with. And for God's sake, put her out of her misery after you've had your pleasure," he said to an infantryman in the act of raping a Shoshoni woman. He could not imagine, though, how anyone could find pleasure in one of these stinking savages. Still, if such activity warmed some men in this miserable cold, well then, let them have it.

And plenty of the men must have been cold, he saw as he rode through the village.

One particularly lithesome young girl lay at the center of a circle of Volunteers; some having taken their turn and others awaiting theirs. The conversation among the men was likewise crude.

The sound of retching diverted the major's attention. He turned in the saddle to see Private John Stevens's head hanging forward over his horse's shoulder, vomit streaming to the ground.

"What's the matter, Stevens? Ain't got the stomach for Indian killing?"

The private looked coldly at the officer as he wiped spew and spittle out of his mustache, then lurched forward as his stomach revolted again. McGarry laughed.

"Stevens, are you going to be any good to me on this mission, or shall I send you back to the river?"

Stevens again swiped his sleeve across his mouth. "It ain't my stomach, Major," he said, hacking to clear his throat. "It's my head."

A blood-soaked bandage wrapped the soldier's head, covering one ear and disappearing under his hat on the other side. A bullet had plowed a furrow along the side of his head during the fighting in the ravine.

"I've got the damndest headache. Keeps giving me the heaves."

That's what he said. But it was, in fact, the actions of the troopers that sickened him. Although few Shoshoni remained in the camp, most by now having fled south across the icy river bottoms or west up Cedar Ridge and the snowy bluffs, those unable to leave were the object of brutal savagery. He saw more than one eviscerated, lying in the snow in puddles of frozen blood and gore. Others with heads split open. One young man appeared to stand slumped against the vertical wall of the ravine. Upon closer inspection, Stevens saw he was pinned there with a bayonet abandoned for the purpose.

As they rode along, they witnessed a trooper tear a baby forcefully from its mother's arms and throw it away as hard as he could, the infant reeling through the air a considerable distance before bouncing, rolling, skidding, sliding across the frozen, trampled ground to finally come to rest against a jumble of rocks at the edge of the ravine.

The soldier then ripped away the top of the woman's dress and shoved her down onto the cold ground, his free hand tugging to unfasten his trousers. Still, the woman resisted, crabbing away on elbows and feet. A blow to the face stopped her but only temporarily. The trooper unholstered his revolver and smashed it against her head. This served only to unleash fury along with her fear, and she dealt him a fierce kick to the crotch.

Gasping for breath, he dropped to one knee in the snow, grasping his pistol in one hand and the woman's ankle in the other to prevent her crawling away. As soon as the pain allowed, he raised the pistol and blasted away the top of the woman's head, then went about his nasty business even as her life ebbed away.

Stevens wondered why the major, or Colonel Connor, did not act to prevent these things. But he wondered, too, why he himself did not voice his displeasure, even going so far as to blame his nausea on a superficial head wound. He sensed the civilian Rockwell shared his disapproval, but the guide did not speak, merely stared grimly at what went on.

By now, they were at the upper reaches of the camp, the area where McGarry, Stevens, and the other cavalry troopers had lately attacked after working their way down the ravine from out of the bluffs. Strewn about were nearly fifty dead Shoshoni warriors who had engaged the dismounted cavalry troopers, then strategically retreated down the ravine only to be caught between McGarry's forces and Holt's infantry soldiers charging through the willows.

"Did you get an estimate of the goods, Rockwell?" McGarry said.

"More or less. I make it half a dozen wagonloads at most."

"You sound confident."

"I've done more than a bit of freighting in my day."

McGarry spent a long moment looking around at the Shoshoni bodies. "I take it you disapprove of these dead, Rockwell," he said, with a nod toward the bodies of the Shoshoni warriors strewn about.

"Not these. Them others. At least these had a chance to fight. Shooting Indians that can shoot back ain't your usual way of doing things, is it?"

"You're a brassy bastard. I could shoot you out of the saddle for disrespectful talk such as that."

"You could try, Major. You could try. I kill better men than you most mornings before breakfast. I ain't et yet, so I'd be happy to oblige whatever you've got in mind."

Stevens could have sworn the heat generated by the encounter between Rockwell and McGarry warmed the very air around them. Had the snow started melting, he would not have been surprised.

The major blinked. He turned in the saddle to talk to the troopers behind him.

"Dismount, men," he said. "Work your way down through the camp. Check every lodge still standing for anything useful. Locate food stores. Blankets. Hides. Consolidate the plunder in a place accessible for loading."

McGarry turned back to Rockwell only to see the guide riding away down the ravine.

Most of the Shoshoni belongings the men gathered seemed to be either given by or stolen from the Mormons, or from emigrant trains. More than half a ton of wheat and flour. Sacks of potatoes. Jerked beef in quantity. Even a sizable flock of chickens. Stacks of buffalo hides and robes, trade blankets. Quilts and blankets of obvious white origin. Stacks of rifles of various vintages and states of repair. Insignificant quantities of lead and powder scattered throughout the camp. Cooking utensils. And nearly two hundred head of horses.

All destined for the auction block at Camp Douglas to cover the cost of the expedition.

A few small parfleches of foodstuffs and the odd blanket were shoved into the hands of lingering Shoshoni, most of which were old women. Food and household goods the soldiers did not like the look of were tossed onto the fires or dumped and scattered in the mud and snow. Brush-covered tipis were fired where they stood; some covers of hide and canvas from other lodges were salvaged, some burned.

Inside one lodge, Private Stevens dragged aside a pile of blankets to reveal a child, a boy no more than two years old. A woman he assumed to be his mother lay face down in the entrance, one shoulder blown apart by a bullet wound and her head split by a blow from an ax. He scooped up the boy, carried him outside, and looked around for the old women still wandering the camp, thinking one of them might care for the baby or know which family he belonged to and where to find them.

"Stevens! What are you doing with that brat?" McGarry hollered from where he sat his horse, supervising the salvage operation. "There's work to be done. And it ain't dandling babies on your knee."

"His mother's dead, sir."

"So? That's nothing to you. Get rid of it."

"Sir?"

"Get rid of it."

"Yessir. I'll just find some squaw to take him."

"Dammit, Stevens, are your ears painted on? I said get rid of it."

"Sir?"

"Kill it, you daft bastard."

Stevens, dumbstruck, merely stared at the major.

"Stevens! Get on with it."

The private still did not respond. McGarry jerked his mount's head around and thumped it in the belly with his bootheels, riding toward Stevens.

"Private!" he yelled, reining up beside Stevens, leaning down so his face was inches from the soldier's. "Will you obey me?"

"Is that an order, sir?"

"Stevens!"

"Sir! Are you ordering me to kill this child?"

"Now, Stevens."

"Is that an order, sir?"

McGarry pulled his revolver, thumbed back the hammer as he shoved the barrel against the back of the child's head, and pulled the trigger. The bullet slammed through the boy, tearing out a chunk of his forehead and barely missing the soldier's head. Stevens dropped the baby as his hands flew involuntarily to his face, wiping away gore, clawing at ringing ears.

The officer holstered his pistol, thought better of it, drew it again, and arced it violently to stop abruptly against the bloody bandage wrapped around the soldier's head, landing near the bullet wound. Stevens collapsed, unconscious.

"That's an order, Private," McGarry said, then turned and rode away.

CHAPTER THIRTY-ONE

A distant wind moans above the bluffs. But here, along the banks of Beaver Creek, the atmosphere is still, suffocating. Even the stench of the aftermath of battle is crushed under a cold blanket of air heavy as ice.

The purity of snow is violated by a kaleidoscope of mislaid color strewn about the ruined campsite: Speckles of brown and yellow and tan from broadcast seeds. Smears of black ash from cooking fires and torched lodges and burned goods. Blue and purple stains from scattered dried berries. Scarlet spills and splashes of blood.

Strange and curious shapes litter the landscape: Torn and tattered cloth twisted and stiff. Slashed, scarred, discarded hides and leather. Lodge skins and canvas, trampled and ragged. Shirts, trousers, dresses, loincloths, shawls, moccasins, deformed and frosted by ice and snow. Contorted horse carcasses in unlikely poses.

And bodies: Grotesque parodies of hundreds of former Shoshoni; babies and boys, girls and women, young men and old; faces distorted in frozen agony, limbs broken and bent at unnatural angles, escaped entrails rigid as ice, pieces and parts of The People, dismembered and dispersed.

And somewhere, up above, a distant wind moans.

Huddled under a cedar tree, weak from pain and loss of blood, Sagwitch sat up and stretched, working the kinks out of his cold joints. This was his fortieth winter on the earth, and each seemed colder and longer than the one before.

The day's light was dying. In the distance he could see greasy smoke rising and the dim glow of garbage fires as the remnants of the Shoshoni winter camp turned to ash. Down near where the road fords the *Boa Ogoi*, he could see where the soldiers were camped, fires blazing high among the small tents pitched on the snowy, frozen ground.

The chief crawled from under the tree's branches and slowly worked his way upright. Both hands reached behind to massage the small of his back as he arched his spine and rotated his shoulders. The bullet wound in his mangled hand had stopped bleeding but still throbbed. His fingers would not work properly, nor could he bend his wrist. The extent of the damage was hard to know; once the blood was washed off and the torn skin cut away, he thought he would be better able to tell how useful it might be once it healed.

But, for now, he put aside thoughts of his aches and injuries and contemplated what he could do to help The People—the few of them still living. He fetched the horse that had carried him from the dying village and swung aboard, not relishing the thought of again crossing the icy stream.

Sagwitch rode due west for a time after the crossing to avoid drawing attention from the soldier camp, then worked his way up and around the face of the bluffs, dropping into Beaver Creek ravine above the camp. He worked his way down to the ruined village. The bodies of his warriors lay thick on the ground, in places piled two and three deep. Many dead women and children lay among them. None of the lodges was standing. Even the poles were gone—fuel, he suspected, for the army's fires.

At the place where his lodge once stood, he found his wife dead on a heap of scorched canvas that had once covered the tipi. Like the woman, the fabric was so bullet riddled the soldiers had set it alight and left it where it fell, but the flames had died like the woman. He rolled her over and there, under her frigid body, he found his infant daughter. She was cold and hungry but still alive, protected from the soldiers and the worst of the chill by her mother's dead body. He rearranged and rewrapped the blankets on the child's cradleboard and carried her along.

He found Bear Hunter. The old war chief slumped awkwardly in the snow, as if he had not been able to decide whether to die sitting up or lying down. Sagwitch tried to stretch the old man into a more comfortable, dignified position, but the body was stiff from cold and rigor, so he abandoned the task. Lehi, too, was dead, he remembered. *I am the only one of the chiefs left,* he realized. It was up to him to lead the people.

From among the refuse, he salvaged enough firewood to kindle a warming blaze on the embers of one of the many dying fires set by the *Toquashes.*

"If there are any more alive," he called out into the darkening day, "come over to my campfire and get dry and warm."

Wet, cold, hungry, demoralized, disheartened, disoriented, a few survivors wandered in. A few more would dribble in as the darkness grew. Most were too old and weak to do much for themselves, others too young. One dazed little boy approached fearfully, still clutching a tiny bowl of pinenut stew, long since frozen solid.

Wounds were many, and the people did what they could to treat their injuries. Sagwitch could see that many of these people would die. There were a few young men—four warriors who had stolen cavalry horses and escaped made their way back to the camp, and a few others came who had fled to safety. The men counseled together to decide what to do.

"We must go to Pocatello and Sanpitch," one said. "When they left the Warm Dance, those people were going back to their own winter encampments. Pocatello will be north, at those hot springs. Maybe Sanpitch and his people will be at that camp in the mountains by the salt lake. They will help us if we join them."

"It is too far," said another. "Some of these people will die before we can get there."

"That is true. We have only a few horses. And the snow is deep. Walking will be hard," said another.

"At least there is not much to carry," the first said with bitter irony.

Sagwitch said, "One thing is for sure—we cannot stay here. I am afraid the solders might come back tomorrow and finish the job. Besides, there is nothing left for us here. We must find help somewhere."

"I think you are wrong about one thing," one of the old men offered. "The soldiers will not come back. Even they are sick of killing."

"But if they knew you were here, Sagwitch, they might come back," said a young man. "I think they would not be happy to know one of our chiefs is still alive."

"Perhaps you are both right," Sagwitch said. "This is what I think. We should gather what food and belongings we can and go to Sanpitch's village. At least some will make it alive, and those who are strong will help the weak. Those who cannot go must be left here. I will go to the Mormons in Franklin and see if I can find help for them."

The chief's suggestion drew surprise and anger from the men.

"The Mormons!" someone said. "Why do you think they will help? They helped the Americans!"

"That is true," said another. "I saw some of those Mormons sitting on the hillside, watching the fight. Maybe they did not fight with the soldiers, but they did not help us."

"Besides," said someone else, "Franklin is where the soldiers will go."

Sagwitch considered what they said, but these were thoughts he himself had already had. He knew the settlers had helped the soldiers. But only some of them. Some of the Mormons were his friends, and he knew they would not approve of what the army had done. Others of the Mormons might kill him or turn him over to the soldiers. But he would be careful and only go to the home of someone he believed he could trust.

He shared his thoughts with the makeshift council. "The strongest must go with you, but some are not able. Those who cannot make it, you must leave behind. I think I can convince some of the Mormons to come for them. If the Mormons will not take them in, they will die. It is unfortunate, but they would die anyway. I see no other way."

The men agreed, reluctantly, because no one could think of a better idea. They would outfit those to be left behind as well as possible, then set out toward the southwest and Sanpitch's camp before the morning.

Since nothing could be done for those already dead, the chief encouraged the strongest of the men to drag as many bodies as possible to the river and dump them in. It was an unfortunate end, but all agreed that, lacking a proper burial, a watery grave was better than leaving the bodies lying on the cold ground to be torn apart by scavengers and scattered across the earth. Not many of the dead, however, made it into the water, despite the best efforts of the survivors. Most of the bodies were left to lie—twisted, contorted carcasses frozen to the icy ground, a blanket of hoar frost glistening in the fading light.

Finally, Sagwitch rewrapped the blankets around his baby daughter for the final time and hung the cradleboard from the branches of a cedar tree. She would be among those left behind. He only hoped she would be given to some white woman who would nurse her and care for her. Otherwise, the baby would die in this place, as had so many others of his family and his people.

Sagwitch climbed on his horse to ride into the cold night toward Franklin. Was it only yesterday, he wondered, that this camp had been a happy place?

Like so much wind-driven sand, desiccated particles of snow stung the exposed skin of The People and irritated the hides of the few horses. Skimpy clothing offered some protection from the blowing snow, but the wind held no respect for the trifling garments. It raged through unabated, and the skin, even the bones, could not slow it much as it seemed to pass through the quivering bodies, then scream away, carrying on its blow whatever heat the human organism could generate.

The rhythm of squeaking, creaking, crunching snow, footstep on footstep, lift and drop, forward ever forward, interrupted from time to time by a trip, a stumble, a lurch, a fall. Curled in the warmth of the snow, the fallen wanted only to stay. They resisted grasping, pulling, lifting, helping hands that wanted only for them to rise and walk some more, buffeted by wind, peppered by rock-hard crystals of frozen water wrung dry.

So much easier to sleep.

But, somewhere ahead, through the parched cold in the direction of the setting sun, glowing fires radiated warmth that eddied around tight lodges, while slow bubbles rose through stews and soups to stretch the surface before the thick bubbles burst, and wisps of aromatic steam drifted lazily upward to smoke holes in the tops of the lodges, only to be ripped away mercilessly by the frigid wind, a wind ignored inside the lodges where warmth lives.

Most of The People who fall, who have fallen before and will fall again, rise each time, driven by the faith, the hope, the

Rod Miller

belief that a pleasant dream, a comforting hallucination, will come true only if the rhythmic song of squeaking, creaking, crunching snow, footstep on footstep, lift and drop, carries them forward, ever forward, long enough to reach relief.

CHAPTER THIRTY-TWO

As the sun struggled over the southeastern horizon, the jingle of trace chains sounded in the cold, misty air above the Bear River. From where he squatted next to a campfire, Colonel Connor looked a ways south on the bluffs to see Porter Rockwell riding down the frozen dugway. Behind him came twelve—no, fourteen—teams, the drivers hauling back on drag brakes trying to keep the big sleighs from running up on the horses.

The colonel snapped off orders, hurrying the soldiers along as they struck the camp. He ordered a cavalry detail to start ferrying the men and supplies across the river, where, again, ice clung to the banks, and the main current flowed thick with ice and slush. The crossing proved less eventful and less exciting than its counterpart of the day before. But the operation proved more somber, as, on this morning, many of the cavalry troopers and foot soldiers ferried across the stream were dead—colder, even, than when soaked and splashed and frozen following yesterday's passage across the Bear River.

The somnolent soldiers labored as if the reality of yesterday's work hung over their shoulders like a blanket of heavy fog. But Connor recognized the need for haste, for if the wounded and frostbitten and chilled and weary men still living did not get away from this place and into more congenial circumstances right away, a good number of them would soon share the fate of the fourteen soldiers stiff and dead under canvas sheets.

Those bodies were the last loads to cross the stream,

suspended precariously in canvas slings stretched between pairs of horses. No soldier, dead or alive, was spilled into the icy water this morning, but cold stacked upon cold from the unavoidable drenched feet and frigid splashes.

Meantime, as the Volunteers stacked booty on the sleighs, packed and stowed and lashed down supplies and camp gear, lifted the wounded and lame into the wagon boxes and flat beds on runners, and finally stacked the dead like so much cordwood in the last of the sleds, a group of settlers was getting about an equally grisly task up on Beaver Creek.

Already informed of the dire situation on the killing field by Porter Rockwell, whose information was supported by the Nelson brothers, then reinforced by the pleading of the wounded Chief Sagwitch, Bishop Preston Thomas had sent a relief party to the Shoshoni at the same time others from his congregation rescued the soldiers. By the time they arrived, the Shoshoni who were able had already bundled up anything worth carrying away and set off toward their people in the Promontory Mountains north of the Great Salt Lake, where Sanpitch kept a winter camp.

But the Mormons did save a few of those left behind. One of the settlers, a tall, gangly redhead named Matt Fifield, detected a rustling in a copse of willows at the river's edge, a ways downstream from where Beaver Creek flowed into the Bear.

"Who's in there?" he said. "C'mon out. No one will hurt you."

No one replied. He spread the thick branches and pawed his way closer to the water.

"Hello! Anybody there?" Still no answer. But, again, he heard rustling and saw the willows quivering just a few feet from where he stood. He snaked his way further in and found a young mother, squatting in knee-deep water that covered her chest deep.

"Hey there," he said softly, trying not to further terrify the frightened woman. "It's all right. I will not hurt you."

The woman finally turned toward him, and he saw that she held a baby, carefully keeping the infant above the surface of the water.

"Good God," Fifield whispered. "Good God."

He extended a hand toward the woman, but she turned away, keeping the baby out of his reach.

"I'll not hurt you, girl. Nor the babe. Come now, it's all over."

Sensing, finally, the absence of threat, the young woman reached out a hand and allowed Fifield to pull her to her feet and lead the way out of the tangled willows but still clutched the baby tightly to herself and would not give it up. Finally, clear of the willows, he scooped up the dripping, shivering woman, baby and all, and carried them to Beaver Creek ravine, where he turned her care over to some women who warmed the pair by a fire and helped her into dry clothing.

"Matt, have you ever seen anything like it?" Ed Nelson asked Fifield.

"I have not, Brother Nelson. I hope never to see anything like it again."

"William Hull and Heber Riley have been all through the village. They stopped counting bodies at two hundred."

"How many living?"

"Three old women. The young one you brought in with the baby. Another baby. Two little boys and a girl. They're all in sorry shape. One of the little boys has three bullet wounds; the girl took one in the thigh. The baby is near frozen."

"There's nothing more we can do here. Let's get them back to town. God help the ones who left. We will pray they find safety somewhere."

The rescuers soon intersected the trail of the sleds hauling the goods plundered from the Shoshoni village, and the sick and wounded California Volunteers. But even had there been no ruts cut into the snow, or a road trampled by the teams, they could have followed the way guided by brilliant red droplets of blood strung out in the wake of the hauling of the wounded.

They stopped on the road and waited as horses separated to stream around and past them—some two hundred captured Shoshoni ponies, driven and hazed and wrangled by cavalry troopers, the drumming of nearly a thousand hooves trembling the earth beneath the Samaritan's feet, then receding into the distance toward the town.

In Franklin, the healthiest of the soldiers were consigned to another night in the open air. But this time, at least, they would sleep inside walls. Bishop Thomas set aside the church tithing yard for the soldier camp, the adobe walls of the enclosure reflecting the warmth of campfires. Hot meals were prepared to rejuvenate the soldiers. Cots and pallets were arranged in the meetinghouse for the wounded, as well as the infantry and cavalry troops who were unable to walk, or nearly so, owing to frozen feet. The most seriously injured, those needing constant nursing, were parceled out among the homes of the town.

But none was sent to the home of John Comish—for that is where Sagwitch hid, receiving care for his shot-up hand.

The farther south the troops traveled, the farther they retreated from the reality of the fight, the more welcome the reception from the Mormon settlers. When the troops arrived in Logan, Peter Maughan was there to greet them. As president of the Mormon church's Cache Valley Stake of Zion, he directed the arrangements for billeting the soldiers and even planned parties and prepared dinners. Major McGarry was able to obtain refills for his clandestine canteens. Tents were pitched on Tabernacle Square. Homes were opened. Women ripped dear fabric for bandages. Maughan sent a crew of workmen south and up into the canyon to clear the road for the coming—leaving—troopers.

Finally, he had it written in church records that "We, the people of Cache Valley, looked upon the movement of Colonel Connor as an intervention of the Almighty, as Indians had been a source of great annoyance to us for a long time, causing us to stand guard over our stock and other property the most of the time since our first settlement."

Thus, the California Volunteers forever left Cache Valley.

CHAPTER THIRTY-THREE

Rockwell disliked hanging around town. The layabout way of life was not to his liking, and he longed for open spaces and fresh air. But since coming back from Bear River he had hardly drawn a breath of country air. It seemed he was always being summoned back to Salt Lake City for one thing or another. The political situation had been dicey. For Rockwell, that meant staying close to Brigham Young.

Territorial officials, led by Governor Stephen Harding, sought to take control of the militia from the Mormons.

Brigham Young ordered Harding and the other federal appointees out of the territory and said, "If they will not resign, and if the president will not remove them, the people must attend to it. I will let him know who is governor. I am governor."

The Mormons got up a petition and sent it to President Lincoln.

Connor followed it with a counter petition, signed by soldiers, officers, and Gentiles.

Brigham Young, on his own authority, armed the Nauvoo Legion—the Mormon militia.

The army called for more troops.

Hundreds, sometimes more than a thousand, of the Saints' sometime soldiers guarded Brigham Young.

Connor blustered but knew he was outnumbered and outgunned, and that his troopers would be used up should it come to a fight.

Federal marshal Isaac Gibbs served a warrant on the church president for violating anti-polygamy laws.

Rockwell escorted Brother Brigham to the courthouse. The president had no cash on hand to go his own bail. Rockwell shelled out.

Through it all, at every opportunity, Rockwell had returned to his ranches to catch up on matters there and see to his express business. And he never passed up a chance to visit his roadhouse near Point of the Mountain, the Hot Springs Brewery Hotel, and sample the wares.

But now, all too soon, here he was back in the city to shop for more horses to haul his freight wagons. He stopped by the Beehive House to report to Brigham Young, hoping his services would not be required and that it would not be necessary to extend his stay.

"Port. It is good to see you," Brigham said from behind his desk. It was late in the evening, but the press of business brought the Mormon leader back to his office after having supper with his wives and children. He muffled a belch and said, "How are you?"

"Wheat. All wheat."

"What brings you back to the city?"

"Express business. How's things with the *federales*?"

"They have settled down somewhat. I think your soldier friends realize their influence here is limited now that we have called up the legion. It is unlikely the army will be reinforced, given the Union's more pressing problems in the east. It is equally unlikely I would allow them to be reinforced.

"And Harding, that thing that is here that calls himself governor—if you were to fill a sack with cow shit, it would be the best thing you could do for an imitation. He may learn to button his lip yet—or we may have to button it for him."

"You think he'll try to prod Connor into doing something stupid?"

"He has tried. And the colonel would like to accommodate. He keeps the telegraph wires sizzling, but I am told his army superiors caution prudence."

"What's been the upshot of the Shoshoni expedition from the army?"

"None that I am aware of. Which means there has been none. Since the initial flurry of felicitations, there has been silence. I suspect Connor's glory is short-lived, and his exploits here will soon be forgotten."

"What's the word from Cache Valley? Some folks up that-away was unhappy when we left. Got what they asked for, I guess, then wished they hadn't asked when they seen the result."

Brigham Young shuffled through a stack of papers on the corner of his desk and withdrew a sheet from the pile. "They seem to be coming to terms with it. I have had a letter from Peter Maughan. He says of the Shoshoni, 'I feel my skirts clear of their blood. They rejected the way of life and salvation which have been pointed out to them from time to time and have thus perished relying on their own strength and wisdom.' "

As he listened to the letter, Rockwell heard with his other ear a horse pounding down Brigham Street. It slid to a stop in front of the office, and he heard excitement pass among the guards stationed outside the door. Someone pounded the door with an urgent fist but did not wait to be invited in.

"Brother Brigham! It's the soldiers!"

"The soldiers? Calm down, man. What are you talking about?"

As the man took a deep breath, anxiety covered his face like a red mask when he realized he had just burst in unannounced on the president of the Church of Jesus Christ of Latter-day Saints.

"Begging your pardon, sir . . . Mister President . . ."

"Brother Brigham. Just call me Brother Brigham. It would seem you have a matter of some urgency to report. Please go on."

"It's the soldiers up at Camp Douglas, sir. They're mustering on the parade ground."

"And?"

"Well, sir, they're armed. They've limbered up cannon. The cavalry is mounted."

"This time of night?" Rockwell said. "Little late for a drill, ain't it? The colonel does like a parade, they say, but it's a little late for that."

"I don't think this is for show. I think they're going to attack."

As if on cue, the sound of artillery fire rolled off the heights and reverberated through the city. The rattle of distant rifle fire rolled down the hill, punctuated again and again by cannon thunder.

"Hell's fire," said Rockwell. "You might be right."

Rockwell summoned a guard detail who knew the routine. Brigham Young was whisked away and within minutes was secure and in hiding. Even before their leader was gone, militia members were converging on his estate from every direction. Pulling on jackets, buttoning shirts, hitching up braces, they came.

As they gathered, Rockwell was taken by the orderliness of it all, each man homing in on his assigned group and falling in to await instructions. Orderly, but anxious. The Nauvoo Legion was, after all, an army of toy soldiers. Organized in Illinois some twenty years ago by the prophet Joseph Smith, the legion had never yet been involved in any military action to speak of, at least not of the fighting kind, save a few forays against Indians. But, like Colonel Patrick Connor, Lieutenant General Joseph

Smith had liked a parade. Killing, for the most part, was always left to men like Rockwell.

Something was missing.

The battle. Rockwell had neither seen nor heard the explosion of a shell; no building had collapsed; nothing was afire. The shooting had stopped. He sought out the legion's ranking officer. There was no further intelligence from the vicinity of Camp Douglas. The man who had burst in on Rockwell and Brigham Young had been the only one assigned there. Lacking any reasonable alternative, Rockwell volunteered to ride to the military camp. He figured it unlikely the soldiers would shoot their erstwhile guide on sight.

By the time he returned, Brigham Young had come out of his hiding place and stood on the porch of the Beehive House. Rockwell rode toward him and reined up at the fence.

"It's a celebration for Colonel Connor," he said. "He got a wire from Halleck, the big soldier back in Washington, praising his 'splendid victory' at Bear River. Only it ain't *Colonel* Connor anymore. It's Brigadier General Connor."

EPILOGUE

31 December 1867

The body was propped upright in the corner of the seedy sleeping room, sitting in a pool of sticky blood, some of which had run down the cracks in the floorboards to drip through the ceiling of the room below, which is what prompted the visit of San Francisco city police officers to room number three-twenty of the Occidental Hotel when the new year of 1868 was mere minutes away.

"How could a man do that to himself?" the young patrolman named Brendan said.

Hopkins, the senior officer, absentmindedly tapped his nightstick against his palm as he studied the scene, squatting before the corpse. They had touched nothing in the room, so he knew the only thing that had changed at the scene was the broken glass on the floor below the transom, where they had broken through to gain access to the room, locked from the inside with the skeleton key jammed into its hole to prevent opening with a master key.

"Wedged himself into that corner, see, to hold his head still," Hopkins said. "Make the cut with less pressure, that way. Fortified himself with some liquid courage, it seems," Hopkins said, with a nod toward two whiskey bottles on the bedside table, one empty and the other likewise, save an inch in the bottom. "Still, he wasn't sure of himself. See them short, shallow cuts on his neck just above there where he finally stuck it in and ripped it

205

across? Like he was trying to make up his mind, you see. Can't say as I blame him. Killin' yourself with a blade ain't the easiest way to get the job done."

"No. I don't mean how. I mean how—I mean why, I guess."

"Couldn't say. Yet," Hopkins said, looking at the knife where it lay in the stiffening puddle of blood, light from the table lamp reflecting off its surface with soft sheen. "Nothing special about that knife. Ordinary pocket knife. Like you can buy anywhere. Kept it sharp, though. See how that blade has been whetted down."

"He must be in the army."

"Used to be. That's an old uniform, see. California Volunteers. From back in the war. Uncle of mine wore one like it. This fellow, though, he was an officer."

They poked around the room, checking the highboy and wardrobe for the man's effects. The police in their inquiries can learn a good deal about a man. But their investigation cannot uncover the despair a man of action feels when action is no longer required of him. Their probing will not reveal the deficiency a man accustomed to the stimulation of danger feels when there is no more danger. Their searches will not divulge the cheapness life holds for one accustomed to death. Nor would their examination disclose that the one and only constant in this man's changed world was an insatiable appetite for whiskey.

No, the police would learn none of this. Still, they searched the premises to know what they could know of the man.

"McGarry," Brendan said, holding up a sheaf of papers pulled from a drawer. "Major Edward F. McGarry."

AUTHOR'S NOTE AND ACKNOWLEDGEMENTS

Although based on historical events and people, *And the River Ran Red: A Novel of the Massacre at Bear River* is a work of fiction, and considerable license has been taken in telling the story.

The names of real Shoshoni, military, and Mormon people associated with the historical events portrayed were borrowed for use by various characters in the story. But those names are *borrowed,* and the specific actions associated with any named character are fictitious. The actions of principal characters—Colonel Patrick Edward Connor, Major Edward F. McGarry, Orrin Porter Rockwell, Brigham Young, Bear Hunter, Sagwitch—are based on historical sources but used fictitiously. Of these principal characters, McGarry is the most obscure, and thus his personality, attitudes, manner of speaking, and demeanor come primarily from the writer's imagination. His fondness for liquor is historical.

Whether or not Bear Hunter, or any other member of his band, witnessed the march of the California Volunteers across the Great Basin or were aware of the killings at Gravelly Ford on the Humboldt River as written here is not known. The meeting of Mormon leaders in which Rockwell informed the brethren of the army's approach is fictional. Various accounts disagree as to the loss of life—if any—during the Van Ornum rescue expedition to Cache Valley. While most Mormon settlers, individually and as a group, were reluctant to assist the soldiers in any way, Rockwell did accompany the Bear River expedition as a guide. His doing so under direct orders of Brigham Young, as represented in these pages, is a product of the writer's imagination, as are Rockwell's methods of persuading churchmen in Cache Valley to lend assistance.

However, it is worth pointing out that one of the most incredible events surrounding the massacre—the cavalry march covering sixty-eight miles in the dead of night and in the face of severe weather—actually occurred.

The military tactics of both the soldiers and the Shoshoni at Beaver Creek are gleaned from historic sources, but those sources do not always agree and are sometimes contradictory. The fighting, as depicted, represents a blending of information from many accounts and the writer's imagination.

Reports of the number of Shoshoni killed in the fight vary widely, but the most well-researched accounts support a minimum number of two hundred-fifty dead, and an upward limit of three hundred-fifty is supportable. Body counts above or below that range cannot be supported by known facts, and many of those claims that say otherwise are based on nonsensical statements. The atrocities featured in the story are fictionalized but based on accounts from Shoshoni sources, reports of soldiers, and Mormon witnesses.

Place names generally reflect those used at the time, which is why Beaver Creek, site of the Shoshoni winter camp, will not be found on modern maps or in most accounts of the massacre. In recognition of events there, from the white settlers' perspective, it was renamed Battle Creek.

At this writing, a couple of roadside monuments are all that mark the massacre site. A highway runs across the path of the cavalry attack and is parallel to and nearly adjacent to where the initial Shoshoni defenses must have been located. The terrain has been altered by floods, fences, canals, irrigation ditches, and land leveling for farming purposes. But maps drawn after the fact by a soldier participant, and since by historians based on historical research, can still be matched in a general way to the site as it appears today.

Efforts at official recognition of the site by state and federal governments have been halting and sporadic and of limited effectiveness. Much of the land where the massacre occurred has now been acquired by the Northwestern Band of the Shoshone Nation. Efforts are ongoing at this writing to acquire more of the land, and to establish a cultural center and interpretive site.

Worth mentioning is that the Timbimboo family, descendants of Sagwitch, have been, and still are at this writing, among the leaders of the Northwestern Band of the Shoshone Nation and have been instrumental in its survival.

Every year, on January 29, the Northwestern Band of the Shoshone Nation, with support and participation by many, many others from all walks of life, congregate at the massacre site in remembrance of their fallen ancestors. But, while these gatherings are solemn occasions, they are not dismal, as the Northwestern Band of the Shoshone Nation are a forward-looking people, more focused on where The People are going, rather than where they have been.

The use of the spelling "Shoshoni" throughout the book is a deliberate choice of the writer based on a belief that it better represents the word's pronunciation. While "Shoshoni" is the choice of many scholars and is an accepted variant, "Shoshone" is more widely used and is, in fact, the spelling used by tribal entities.

While not to be blamed for the writer's interpretations in telling this story, or in a previous nonfiction book, *Massacre at Bear River—First, Worst, Forgotten*, several books provided most of the historical detail on which they rely. Most helpful were two works by the late eminent historian Brigham D. Madsen: *The Shoshoni*

Frontier and the Bear River Massacre and *Glory Hunter—A Biography of Patrick Edward Connor.*

Other information enriching the Shoshoni perspective came from Mae Parry's writings in *A History of Utah's American Indians,* edited by Forrest S. Cuch, and *Sagwitch,* by Scott R. Christensen.

Harold Schindler's biography *Orrin Porter Rockwell: Man of God / Son of Thunder,* remains the definitive work on that subject. Schindler also authored a most helpful magazine article, "The Bear River Massacre: New Historical Evidence" that appeared in the Fall, 1999, issue of *Utah Historical Quarterly* and includes a recently discovered (at the time) first-hand account by a participating soldier of the California Volunteers.

Other helpful sources in book form include *The Forgotten Kingdom* by David L. Bigler, *The Civil War in the American West* by Alvin M. Josephy, Jr., *The Saints and the Union* by E. B. Long, and *A History of Cache County* by F. Ross Peterson.

Numerous other sources of information were accessed via the Internet, including facts about the Bear River from the United States Geological Survey, and the State of Utah Natural Resources, Division of Water Resources, web sites. General information about the massacre and the time period was gathered from the web sites of the Utah State Historical Society and Idaho State Historical Society. A brief report of the death of Major Edward McGarry was located in an archived San Francisco City Directory on the USGenWeb project.

The information gleaned from these and other sources was essential in providing general and specific information, but mistakes in interpretation, misreading, inaccuracies, or any other errors or misrepresentations of historical facts—whether intended for dramatic purposes or inadvertent—are the responsibility of the writer of this work of fiction.

AND THE RIVER RAN RED

Bitter wind cries out of a moonless sky,
canteens freeze to ice.
Horses stagger on, seventy miles by dawn;
victory comes at a price.

Drumbeats pound, songs resound
on cliffs above the river banks,
a Warm Dance to bring in an early spring,
and send the Great Spirit thanks.

And the river ran red
rolling with the bodies of the dead
massacred on the banks of the River Bear.
Blue-coated soldiers carried out killing orders there
and the river ran red.

Hoofs test the edge of the bluff ledge
to the banks of the Bear below.
And the splash freezes quick and ice floats thick
in the black of the river's flow.

Before the sun, before night is done,
brass bugles sound the attack.

Through Beaver Creek ravine rolled the killing
  machine
and there was no turning back.

And the river ran red
rolling with the bodies of the dead
massacred on the banks of the River Bear.
Blue-coated soldiers carried out killing orders there
and the river ran red.

No surrender, no quarter,
now blood forever stains her shore.
With bayonet and gun, when their work was
  done,
three hundred Shoshoni breathed no more.

And the river ran red
rolling with the bodies of the dead.
And the river ran red.

*From the album *Rocky Mountain Drifter* by Brenn Hill; Defenders Recording Company, ©2018. Music by Brenn Hill; lyrics by Brenn Hill and Rod Miller.

212

ABOUT THE AUTHOR

Writer **Rod Miller** is a four-time winner of, and six-time finalist for, the Western Writers of America Spur Award. His writing has also won awards from Western Fictioneers, Westerners International, and the Academy of Western Artists. A lifelong Westerner, Miller writes fiction, history, poetry, and magazine articles about the American West's people and places. Read more online at writerRodMiller.com, RawhideRobinson.com, and writerRodMiller.blogspot.com.

The employees of Five Star Publishing hope you have enjoyed this book.

Our Five Star novels explore little-known chapters from America's history, stories told from unique perspectives that will entertain a broad range of readers.

Other Five Star books are available at your local library, bookstore, all major book distributors, and directly from Five Star/Gale.

Connect with Five Star Publishing

Visit us on Facebook:
https://www.facebook.com/FiveStarCengage

Email:
FiveStar@cengage.com

For information about titles and placing orders:
(800) 223-1244
gale.orders@cengage.com

To share your comments, write to us:
Five Star Publishing
Attn: Publisher
10 Water St., Suite 310
Waterville, ME 04901